More Praise for *Flash Fiction International*

"These sometimes brilliant, often cunning, always intriguing very short stories fit the moment, the Web, the world we live in now. A stunning flock of lovely and compelling pieces by wonderful writers from all over the world—it's a remarkable and remarkably readable collection."
—Frederick Barthelme, editor of *New World Writing*

"An illuminating world tour of literary bobby-dazzlers!"
—Bobbie Ann Mason, author of *The Girl in the Blue Beret*

"These bursts of illumination, some less than a page long—evoking shock, wonder, laughter, all with a tantalizing sense of completion—establish flash fiction on a global scale. An incomparable set of stories, this book is a new landmark anthology for the *very* short story form."
—Jane Ciabattari, BBC book columnist

"This is the first major international anthology devoted to flash fiction—and it is very impressive. Rich, eclectic, and of the highest caliber."
—Peter Blair and Ashley Chantler, editors of *Flash: The International Short-Short Story Magazine*, UK

"Tiny superb stories, no words wasted. And don't miss the Flash Theory section at the end!"
—Susan Bernofsky, director of literary translation at Columbia University

"Like the most diligent of cultural anthropologists, the editors of *Flash Fiction International* have sifted through centuries of micro art to record and then exhibit these enduring small stories, common in their humanity but culturally distinct in their presentations. This anthology is a gift to the literary community, an important contribution to the understanding of the flash species in all its variegated forms."
—Tara L. Masih, editor of *The Rose Metal Press Field Guide to Writing Flash Fiction*

FLASH
FICTION
INTERNATIONAL

Very Short Stories
from Around the World

EDITED BY

JAMES THOMAS
ROBERT SHAPARD
CHRISTOPHER MERRILL

W. W. NORTON & COMPANY

New York London

For information about special discounts for bulk purchases, please
contact W. W. Norton Special Sales at specialsales@wwnorton.com or
800-233-4830

Manufacturing by Courier Westford
Book design by JAM Design
Production manager: Louise Mattarelliano

Library of Congress Cataloging-in-Publication Data

Flash fiction international : very short stories from around the world
/ edited by James Thomas, Robert Shapard, Christopher Merrill. —
First edition.
pages cm
Includes bibliographical references.
ISBN 978-0-393-34607-7 (pbk.)
1. Short stories. 2. Fiction—20th century. 3. Fiction—21st century.
I. Thomas, James, 1946– editor. II. Shapard, Robert, 1942– editor.
III. Merrill, Christopher, editor.
PN6120.2.F63 2015
808.83'1—dc23
                                            2014043259

W. W. Norton & Company, Inc.
500 Fifth Avenue, New York, N.Y. 10110
www.wwnorton.com

W. W. Norton & Company Ltd.
Castle House, 75/76 Wells Street, London W1T 3QT

1 2 3 4 5 6 7 8 9 0

We could not have made this book without our faithful associate editors, who did a wonderful job of reading, rating, and commenting on countless flash fictions from around the world: Margaret Bentley, Michelle Elvy, D. Seth Horton, P. J. Jones, Tara Laskowski, David Lemming, Michael Malone, Kristina Reardon, Denise Robinow, Ethel Rohan, Andy Root, Revé Shapard, and Michelle Shin.

CONTENTS

Contents

INTRODUCTION

WHAT'S FLASH FICTION called in other countries? In Latin America it may be a *micro*, in Denmark a *kort-prosa*, in Bulgaria a *mikro razkaz*. Some are only a paragraph long, others two pages (they're all very short stories, some very, very short), but such measurements don't tell us much. We prefer metaphors like Luisa Valenzuela's:

> I usually compare the novel to a mammal, be it wild as a tiger or tame as a cow; the short story to a bird or a fish; the micro story to an insect (iridescent in the best cases).

These iridescent insects have been gaining in popularity for more than two decades. In the United States, anthologies, collections, and chapbooks have sold about a million copies. Not as many as some bestsellers, but notable nonetheless. Professional actors have read them to live audiences on Broadway, their performances taped for airing on National Public Radio. In Switzerland, Spain, and Argentina, *minificción* world congresses have been held; in Thailand and the Philippines, flash world seminars have met. A national Flash Fiction Academy has been established in China. Most recently, National Flash Fiction Days were declared in Great Britain and New Zealand.

Having had something to do with the popularity of flash ourselves, in publishing the first *Flash Fiction*, in 1992, then *Flash Fiction Forward*, in 2005, naturally we've been eager to bring you a new book of the best very short stories in the world. But we needed the right opportunity. A few years ago, collecting Latin American stories for *Sudden Fiction Latino*, we spent more than a year searching libraries, bookstores, and the Internet, but that was a project on a different scale. All six continents seemed out of reach, until we were joined by Christopher Merrill, who is director of the University of Iowa's International Writing Program, and a widely published poet and writer of flash fiction.

Chris convinced us to see not just through American eyes but to widen our vision. When we launched the project, corresponding with hundreds of writers and translators around the world, we asked them for ideas—which they generously sent, with further contacts.

Flash fiction began to pour in, most recognizable as stories, though some were highly unusual or fantastic. Flash has always been a form of experiment, of possibility. Here were stories based on musical or mathematical forms, a novel in a paragraph, a scientific report of volcanic fireflies that proliferate in nightclubs. We were open to anything, including contemporary Australian Aboriginal tales (they were short enough, but seemed made to be chanted—were they flash?) and ancient Mayan rituals (at least the *translations* were new). And those Sumerian clay tablets, vivid with laughter and jealousy and the poetry of domestic life? They might be accepted as a flash today by an Internet magazine. They weren't for us, yet reminded us that flash wasn't born on the Internet.

Yet we can't deny that flash has flourished far more quickly and widely, has become far more a part of the world by means of the Internet than we ever imagined. As one editor of Chinese flash fiction has noted, being "device-independent and compatible with today's technology" has allowed flash a "freedom from censorship not enjoyed in other media." Beyond the United States, family or village stories may include more extended family, and be more satirical; intimate or personal stories edge toward philosophy or the world of ideas. As for the idea of flash itself, the rest of the world seems more interested in talking about the nature, purpose, and meaning of flash, while in the United States the focus has been on the creative and practical, that is, how to write it.

But why talk *about* flash at all? For the same reason we talk about any art—to enjoy, to share, to understand ourselves and our culture—and because ideas are powerful. We began to ask authors and translators for their favorite brief quote about flash, and replies came from around the world. Many of them cited American thinkers and authors—they had been reading *us* as well. In fact a world conversation has been going on related to flash. We offer some of it at the end of this anthology in a section called "Flash Theory"—big ideas in tiny spaces, as short as a sentence (whether deep, outrageous, humorous, or in the best cases iridescent).

Finally, the question a reader of any anthology should ask, *Why these particular stories?* We selected the best, not trying for the widest representation, and giving hardly any thought to subject matter. Since "the best," in literature, is always to some degree subjective, we recruited a community to help us keep our view from being too narrow, a dozen associate readers different in genders, ages, and walks of life—mostly writers who were also something else—baker, lawyer, vice president of a university, honkytonk owner. All of them loved to read. We sent batches of flash fiction to each other and kept in touch by email—from Bali to Hawaii to Utah to Texas to Ohio to Virginia to Connecticut—with calculated ratings and unruly comments. We agreed to include a few classics because we liked that they extend and deepen our idea of flash, and because they are among the best flashes ever.

At last, ten thousand stories later, our deadline at hand, we made our final cuts, and herein offer you eighty-six of the world's best very short stories—known in Portuguese as *minicontos*, in German as *Kürzestgeschichten*, in Irish as *splancfhicsin*, in Italian as *microstorias* . . . and in English as *flash fiction*.

As always, our thanks to Amy Cherry, our editor at W. W. Norton, and our agent, Nat Sobel, of Sobel Weber Associates in New York.

We also wish to thank all the individuals and organizations who generously helped in our research for this book—it would be impossible to name them all. But some deserve special recognition: the University of Iowa's International Writing Program (IWP), including Lisa DuPree, Hugh Ferrer, and Ashley Davidson; former IWP participants Alvin Pang, in Singapore, and Kyoko Yoshida, in Tokyo; also at the University of Iowa, Jennifer Feely in Chinese Literature, and Nataša Durovicová of the MFA program in Literary Translation. At the Center for Translation Studies at the University of Texas at Dallas, Charles Hatfield, George Henson, and María Rosa Suárez. For the American Literary Translators Association, Gary Racz and Russell Valentino. At the Asia Pacific Writers and Translators Organisation, Jane Camens. Susan Bernofsky, Director of Literary Translation at Columbia University. We also want to thank the Geyers, the staff of the Olive Kettering Library at Antioch College, and the staff on the Special Collections Floor, Memorial Library, University of Wisconsin. And, not least, our permissions person, Margaret Gorenstein, who is the best.

FLASH
FICTION
INTERNATIONAL

The Story, Victorious

Etgar Keret

THIS STORY IS the best story in the book. More than that, this story is the best story in the world. And we weren't the ones to come to that conclusion. It was also reached by a unanimous team of dozens of unaffiliated experts who—employing strict laboratory standards—measured it against a representative sampling taken from world literature. This story is a unique Israeli innovation. And I bet you're asking yourselves, how is it that we (tiny little Israel) composed it, and not the Americans? What you should know is that the Americans are asking themselves the same thing. And more than a few of the bigwigs in American publishing stand to lose their jobs because they didn't have that answer at the ready while it still mattered.

Just as our army is the best army in the world—same with this story. We're talking here about an opening so innovative that it's protected by registered patent. And where is this patent registered? That's the thing, it's registered in the story itself! This story's got no shtick to it, no trick to it, no touchy-feely bits. It's forged from a single block, an amalgam of deep insights and aluminum. It won't rust, it won't bust, but it may wander. It's supercontemporary, and timelessly literary. Let History be the judge! And by the way, according to many fine folk, judgment's been passed—and our story came up aces.

"What's so special about this story?" people ask out of innocence or ignorance (depending on who's asking). "What's it got that isn't in Chekhov or Kafka or I-don't-know-who?" The answer to that question is long and complicated. Longer than the story itself, but less complex. Because there's nothing more intricate than this story. Nevertheless, we attempt to answer by example. In contrast to works by Chekhov and Kafka, at the end of this story, one lucky winner—randomly selected from among all the correct readers—will receive a brand-new Mazda Lantis with a metallic gray finish. And from among the incorrect readers, one special someone will be selected to receive another car, cheaper, but no less impressive in its metallic grayness so that he or she shouldn't feel bad. Because this story isn't here to condescend. It's here so that you'll feel good. What's that saying printed on the place mats at the diner near your house? ENJOYED YOURSELF—TELL YOUR FRIENDS! DIDN'T ENJOY YOURSELF—TELL US! Or, in this case—report it to the story. Because this story doesn't just tell, it also listens. Its ears, as they say, are attuned to every stirring of the public's heart. And when the public has had enough and calls for someone to put an end to it, this story won't drag its feet or grab hold of the edges of the altar. It will, simply, stop.

Translated by Nathan Englander

The Story, Victorious, II

But if one day, out of nostalgia, you suddenly want the story back, it will always be happy to oblige.

Please Hold Me
the Forgotten Way

H. J. Shepard

H IS HAIR WAS dark and soft and curled a little because
it was getting long. He must have thought it made
him look too pretty. He disliked anything that made him
attractive. He asked her to shave it. She liked the hair. She
imagined touching it with her fingers and coming away
with the sweet dark smell of his scalp on her hands. He left
his wool hat at her house one night and she had slept with
it next to her face. She hated giving it back, and crawled
around her blankets at night trying to catch his smell as it
disappeared.

She knew the drive to his house. She knew the trees she
would pass, the fire hydrants, the dogs barking behind their
fences. She knew where she would park, where the tires
would hit the curb. She knew the way she would breathe
and straighten her skirt, and the feel of the heat that would
prickle down her arms and explode in her fingertips when
she saw him through the kitchen window, coming to the
door. He usually stared her down. Big dark eyes that studied
her like a rare specimen. It wasn't exactly an adoring gaze. It

was more one of bewilderment and concern. He greeted her like this the day she came to shave his head. He opened the door very cordially, one hand behind his back like the head-waiter at a French restaurant, bowing slightly. She sensed his hand brush gently against her back as she came in. She moved too quickly for it to rest there.

"I have everything ready," he said severely, as if she had arrived to perform some critical operation.

She sat down at his kitchen table and smiled at him. The cold winter sunlight pooled in through the window and lit her hands folded on her lap, and she hoped he would remember her like this when he was an old man.

They went down the stairs out of the sunny kitchen and he followed close behind her. The bathroom in the basement was cold and lit by fluorescent lights. He knelt in front of her, and she thought that with him on his knees like this she could either love him or kill him. She could hold his head tenderly against her belly, or break his neck with one quick move. She could do both of these things with her hands.

The razor looked comical to her when she picked it up, hot pink against the cracked cement walls of the bathroom that were painted a dark fungal green. She ran the faucet. Waited for the water to heat up. Waited for it to be just right. She moved her wet soapy hands gently around his head, soaking his hair, around his ears, across his temples, to the nape of his neck. Some of it dripped down his face and he let it run to his chin and fall to the floor. She took the hair from his head in clumps, trying to ignore his back pressed against her legs, lifting and falling with his breath. And when she had washed the soap away his head was like a smooth ostrich egg. Porcelain white, shining and bare. His eyebrows stood out like black coal marks, alone on his face.

And she caught her breath when she saw the two of

them in the mirror. The fluorescent light made their faces a sickly pale green and their eyes were underlined by dark circles. They both looked so tired. He looked sick and cold, and she looked as if she had been crying for him for a very long time.

~~~

Prisoner of War

Muna Fadhil

FOR MARCIA LYNX

S AHIRA WAS STANDING in the doorframe, watching her father grow transparent as the morning sun glowed in her bleach-white kitchen. He sat at the marble table, gutting a radio transistor. The sun washed right through him. Sahira reached out for him, but Saleh shrugged away and disappeared like a mirage against the white walls.

Saleh was constantly amazed by the electronic gadgets around him. They looked nothing like they had when he was first caught by the Iranians twenty years before. Now, he spent most of his days discovering them. In captivity, everything had been the same. Prisoners exchanged the same stories for the hundredth time and pretended to be hearing them afresh. Sahira smiled at him. He looked like a little boy, consumed by the task at hand. She walked to the sink to wash and drain her greens.

Sahira had been five when Saleh was captured, twenty-three when he was released. Sahira and her mother waited as the first, second, and third round of prisoners of war exchanged between Iraq and Iran, long after the end of the eight-year war. They asked returning prisoners if they had met Saleh, if they had known him. No one had. Sahira's mother died in 1996. Saleh made it out in 1998.

That winter, Sahira slept three nights in her car at Al Nusoor Square in Baghdad, where it was promised the last of the POWs would be brought home. Sahira brought an old ID photo of her father, which she'd enlarged and put in a bright gold frame. Sahira hoped that, even if Saleh didn't recognize her, he'd at least recognize his old self. Sahira slouched down in the seat of her car, pulled her sleeves to cover her cold fingertips, and dozed off. She woke up when her car began rocking as people squeezed past it in the mayhem. The crowds made her car move with them.

At first, Saleh didn't believe it when the prison doors flung open and the guards yelled at them in Farsi to get out. Saleh thought, as his cellmates did, that they would be executed. "Do you think they're letting us go?" one hopeful man asked. "Shut up!" Saleh slapped him. They walked them outside, single file. The outside world was blindingly bright. Saleh was hungry to see sky, but it was brighter than his eyes could handle. When they threw new clothes at them and told them to change, Saleh began to wonder. He tore off a strip of his old shirt and hid it: if this was false hope, he was going to strangle himself. Then Saleh and the others were put in buses that had padded seats. Saleh had not sat on a cushion in eighteen years. He pushed the palms of his hands into the padding and cried. He knew then that they were going home.

"Bushra!"

"Daddy! Here!" They embraced and lost track of time. The crowds roared around them.

"Bushra!" Saleh was about to kiss Sahira on the lips.

"Daddy, it's me, Sahira. Mommy she . . ." Sahira hesitated. Saleh pulled his arms off his daughter as though he'd been electrocuted. Sahira, his tiny girl who'd clung to his leg, giggling and shaking her curly hair as he swung his leg up and down, walking across a room. "Sahira." Saleh placed a kiss on her forehead. "I didn't recognize you."

"Daddy?" Saleh looked up as Sahira dried her hands on a towel. "Lunch is ready for when you're hungry. All you have to do is heat it. OK? I have to go to work. Do you need anything? OK? OK." Sahira had her usual one-sided conversation. She patted his head as she walked past him to grab her coat and purse. "Don't leave the house, OK? And call me if you need anything."

Saleh was too consumed by the radio's inner workings to be bothered. Saleh heard the sound of the bolt once, then twice, and then his daughter's footsteps moving away. Saleh carefully reached down to feel if the padding in the chair under him was real. He then got up and closed the curtains to block out the blinding sun.

The Waterfall

Alberto Chimal

THEY HOLD THE baby above the baptismal font, small and fragile, his head still naked. He's awake: he feels the moisture, senses the cold that pierces the stone even though he doesn't know them or know what to call them. But the parents, all of a sudden, seem undecided. Seconds go by. The priest looks at them. And we, piled on top of each other, interrupting each other with trembling whispers, hesitate; speculate. What will they do? Will they name him (after all) Hermenegildo? Will they name him Óscar, Diocleciano, Ramachandra? Piotr? Leonardo? Humberto, Lloyd, Sabú, Carlos, Antonio, Werner, François, Pendelfo, Abderramán, Fructuoso, Berengario, Clodomiro, Florian, Jasón, Guglielmo, Lee, Clark Kent, Martin Luther, Rocambole, Cthulhu . . . ?

—Mauricio—they say.

—What?

—They said Mauricio.

—Mauricio?

—And Alberto. As a matter of fact, Mauricio Alberto.

—Mauricio Alberto?

—What did they say?—and some don't want to believe it, they hesitate in their disbelief, but it's true: the water flows from the bowl over the so very young skin, and we all fall with it, we're all desperate, all wanting to swim with at least an illusion of tiny arms and legs, with body strength and a real body, and since we don't have one we have no other choice but to go down, faster and faster, until we land on his forehead that doesn't understand anything, which only the most detestable Mauricio and the cur Alberto are able to hold on to with the claws the rite gave them, and become a brand on his body, and become the child, and they look at the rest of us while we slide, rejected; while we return, all of us, Óscar, Diocleciano, Ramachandra, Piotr, Leonardo, Humberto, Lloyd, Sabú, Carlos, Antonio, Werner, François, Pendelfo, Abderramán, Fructuoso, Berengario, Clodomiro, Florian, Jasón, Guglielmo, Lee, Clark Kent, Martin Luther, Rocambole, Cthulhu, Peter, Terencio, Goran, Emil, Cuauhtli, all us names that return to the tiny waterfall toward the bottom of the font, the bottom of memories and possibilities, to sleep until the next ceremony.

Mauricio means "dark" and Alberto mean "bright": the choice, we tell ourselves, has its poetry:

—Even though they sound horrible together.

—Appalling.

—They're going to make him unlucky!—Belerofonte shouts, but the parents and Mauricio Alberto, who are leaving now, can't hear us. Our voices are the murmur of splashing water. Down, deep inside the darkness, dreams and monsters beat.

Translated by George Henson

Eating Bone

Shabnam Nadiya

DISHA HADN'T WALKED out of the house in anger, she never did. She waited until some time had passed, wrapped her sari around herself neatly, pulled her hair into the accustomed knot, though tighter than usual, checked her purse and mumbled something about going to see her tailor. Her husband didn't bother looking up from the television.

"It's over," Disha said aloud. *"Shesh."* The juddering movement of the rickshaw made her voice shake on that last word, as if there was still some uncertainty left. Ten years of marriage; ten, a nice, rounded number, ten, without any children. Who knew why. Beyond gossip, complaints and allegations, the childlessness was unexplored.

As she descended from the rickshaw at a random street corner, she recalled this morning's taunt. It was a new one. Disha knew all his usual jibes: her fleshy belly and sagging breasts, her barrenness, her dark skin, her unkempt domesticity, her lack of property. What was she good for?

And now this one: all he had to say was *Talaaq*, three times, and Disha would be divorced, out of the house.

She kept silent about the newspaper article that said saying *Talaaq* thrice wasn't all it took, these days the law demanded more effort if a man wanted to rid himself of a wife. She kept silent about how the sordidness and uncertainty of marriage for women should be left unsaid in their kind of household, that this was something her maid might hear from her husband, but not someone like Disha in the air-conditioned splendor of her posh neighborhood.

As she walked, the strong aroma of roasting chicken invaded her nostrils. The smell spoke to her, as if the tendrils of smoke wisping in the air were messengers, entering her head through her nose, leaving indiscreet messages. She salivated as she looked at the glass-cased spit at the eatery. It was set right in front of the café, almost on the sidewalk. The chickens skewered into inert lines by thick steel rods turned relentlessly as she watched, fat dripping from them. A young boy stood next to it, beside him a small table with some bottles and chopping paraphernalia. Stacked in a corner near his feet were plastic boxes and bundles of fabric bags. All the things required to prepare a roasted chicken for a customer to take away without even having to go inside the café.

He caught her staring and began his litany immediately. "Shall I get you one, *apa*? They're beautifully done by now, and I'll spice them up the way you love. You've been here before, you've had our chicken. I remember you. Take one; I'll throw in some extra salad."

Disha sat on her bed, naked, her breasts hanging slackly brown, chocolate-nippled. She ripped open the dirty-white box of thin plastic that sat between her spread-out legs, and gazed at the spice-browned chicken as it lay on its back, legs splayed, dead yet inviting.

The dying afternoon sun directed spent rays here and there, and the golden hue surprised her as one landed on her fleshy thigh. The chicken felt heavenly in her mouth, her taste buds flaring at the saltiness and hotness and the sweet-sour tang of chili sauce. The fat hadn't completely dripped away during the slow burning, and some dribbled down her chin, now landing on her belly. Disha didn't bother wiping it off as her jaw moved continuously.

There was no other food in the house today, Disha had cooked nothing. Her husband stood at the bedroom door, slack-jawed, transfixed at the vision of her. The meat was finished and she stared at the small heap of bones in front of her. She remembered her mother eating chicken: how the woman had loved to crunch the bones! The best chewable bones, she would tell her daughter, were in the bits no one wanted. And so Ma would eat neck, tail, feet, head. But not Disha: she had eaten flesh, now she would eat bone. She picked up one of the bigger bones and licked the knob on the end. She would eat it all. Today she would eat the world.

Esse

Czesław Miłosz

LOOKED AT THAT face, dumbfounded. The lights of *métro* stations flew by; I didn't notice them. What can be done, if our sight lacks absolute power to devour objects ecstatically, in an instant, leaving nothing more than the void of an ideal form, a sign like a hieroglyph simplified from the drawing of an animal or bird? A slightly snub nose, a high brow with sleekly brushed-back hair, the line of the chin—but why isn't the power of sight absolute?—and in a whiteness tinged with pink two sculpted holes, containing a dark, lustrous lava. To absorb that face but to have it simultaneously against the background of all spring boughs, walls, waves, in its weeping, its laughter, moving it back fifteen years, or ahead thirty. To have. It is not even a desire. Like a butterfly, a fish, the stem of a plant, only more mysterious. And so it befell me that after so many attempts at naming the world, I am able only to repeat, harping on one string, the highest, the unique avowal beyond which no power can attain: *I am, she is*. Shout, blow the trumpets, make thousands-strong marches, leap, rend your clothing, repeating only: *is!*

She got out at Raspail. I was left behind with the immensity of existing things. A sponge, suffering because it cannot saturate itself; a river, suffering because reflections of clouds and trees are not clouds and trees.

Translated by Czesław Miłosz
and Robert Pinsky

The Gospel of Guy No-Horse

Natalie Diaz

At The Injun That Could, a jalopy bar drooping and lopsided on the bank of the Colorado River—a once mighty red body now dammed and tamed blue—Guy No-Horse was glistening drunk and dancing fancy with two white gals—both yellow-haired tourists still in bikini tops, freckled skins blistered pink by the savage Mohave Desert sun.

Though The Injun, as it was known by locals, had no true dance floor—truths meant little on such a night—card tables covered in drink, ash, and melting ice had been pushed aside, shoved together to make a place for the rhythms that came easy to people in the coyote hours beyond midnight.

In the midst of Camel smoke hanging lower and thicker than a September monsoon, No-Horse rode high, his PIMC-issued wheelchair transfigured—a magical chariot drawn by two blond, beer-clumsy palominos perfumed with coconut sunscreen and dollar-fifty Budweisers. He was as careful as any man could be at almost 2 a.m. to avoid their sunburned toes—in the brown light of The Injun, chips in their toenail polish glinted like diamonds.

Other Indians noticed the awkward trinity and gath-

ered round in a dented circle, clapping, whooping, slinging
obscenities from their tongues of fire: Ya-ha! Ya-ha! Jeer-
ing their dark horse, No-Horse, toward the finish line of an
obviously rigged race.

No-Horse didn't hear their rabble, which was soon over-
powered as the two-man band behind the bar really got
after it—a jam probably about love, but maybe about freedom, and definitely about him, as his fair-haired tandem, his
denim-skirted pendulums kept time. The time being now—

No-Horse sucked his lips, imagined the taste of the white
girls' thrusting hips. *Hey!* He sang. *Hey!* He smiled. *Hey!* He
spun around in the middle of a crowd of his fellow tribesmen,
a sparkling centurion moving as fluid as an Indian could be
at almost two in the morning, rolling back, forth, popping
wheelies that tipped his big head and swung his braids like
shiny lassos of lust. The two white gals looked down at him,
looked back up at each other, raised their plastic Solo cups-
runneth-over, laughing loudly, hysterical at the very thought
of dancing with a broken-down Indian.

But about that laughter, No-Horse didn't give a damn.
This was an edge of rez where warriors were made on nights
like these, with music like this, and tonight he was out, dancing at The Injun That Could. If you'd seen the lightning of
his smile, not the empty space leaking from his thighs, you
might have believed that man was walking on water, or at
least that he had legs again.

And as for the white girls slurring around him like two
bedraggled angels, one holding on to the handle of his
wheelchair, the other spilling her drink all down the front of
her shirt, well, for them he was sorry. Because this was not a
John Wayne movie, this was The Injun That Could, and the
only cavalry riding this night was in No-Horse's veins. *Hey!*
Hey! Hey! he hollered.

Man Carrying Books

Linh Dinh

I T IS TRUE that a man carrying a book is always accorded a certain amount of respect, if not outright awe, in any society, whether primitive or advanced. Knowing this fact, Pierre Bui, an illiterate bicycle repairman from the village of Phat Dat, deep in the Mekong Delta, took to carrying a book with him wherever he went.

Its magic became manifest instantaneously: beggars and prostitutes were now very reluctant to accost him, muggers did not dare to mug him, and children always kept quiet in his presence.

Pierre Bui only carried one book at first, but then he realized that with more books, he would make an even better impression. Thus he started to walk around with at least three books at a time. On feast days, when there were large crowds on the streets, Pierre Bui would walk around with a dozen books.

It didn't matter what kinds of books they were—*How to Win Friends and Influence People, Our Bodies, Ourselves, Under the Tuscan Sun*, etc.—as long as they were books. Pierre Bui did seem particularly fond of extremely thick books with tiny print, however. Perhaps he thought they were more scholarly? In his rapidly growing library one could find many tomes on accounting and white pages of all the world's greatest cities.

The cost of acquiring so many books was not easy on Pierre Bui's tiny bicycle repairman's salary. He had to cut out all of his other expenses except for food. There were many days when he ate nothing but bread and sugar. In spite of this Pierre Bui never sold any of his precious volumes. The respect accorded him by all the other villagers more than compensated for the fact that his stomach was always growling.

Pierre Bui's absolute faith in books was rewarded in 1972 when, during one of the fiercest battles of the war, all the houses of his village were incinerated except for his leaning grass hut, where Pierre Bui squatted trembling but essentially unscathed, surrounded by at least ten thousand books.

The Attraction of Asphalt

Stefani Nellen

MOTHER AND DAUGHTER drive up the switchbacks to the Heiligenberg to get spring water, because black tea tastes best with spring water. Plastic canisters tumble over on the backseat as the car takes the curves. The daughter, Martina, fingers her seat belt. She imagines the canisters are alive, thirsty comic book monsters yearning for moisture.

The mother says, "If I told you to jump out of the car because we're going to have an accident, how fast could you do it?" She stares ahead, wrestles the steering wheel, muscles working under her tan skin.

"Come on," she says, "I want to know. If I said, jump out now, what would you do?"

Martina's hands grow hot. The heat travels up her arms, into her chest and tummy. "I don't know."

The mother presses the accelerator. The switchbacks become narrower and steeper, like arrowheads pointing in a new direction each moment. One of the canisters falls to the floor. The mother's palms slap against the leather of the steering wheel. She blows a strand of hair from the corner of her mouth and accelerates more.

Martina says, "I'd open the door and jump out and protect my head."

The mother nods. "And don't forget the seat belt. Take it off first."

"I will."

"And jump away from the car. The door could hit you and push you under the car. You don't want that."

"No." Martina sweats. Sunrays flicker dangerous messages through the leaves. She imagines opening the door. Branches snap past. The air pulls the handle out of her hand. She jumps out. Asphalt and gravel tear at her skin. Tires screech. She can't imagine the sound of a car crashing into a tree. Do trees feel pain? Only if their roots are hurt. Otherwise, they grow new branches.

The mother says, "Ready?"

The seat belt buckle burns the girl's palm. The strap bites into the side of her neck. She tightens her grip on the buckle, puts her thumb on the release. "Ready."

"Good." The mother nods at the road, at the ghosts she sees. "Good. You need to be prepared."

The girl clutches the seat belt, waits for her mother to yell, "Jump!" She waits curve after curve, all the way up the mountain, until her mother pulls up next to the mountain spring and stops the engine and thuds her fists against the steering wheel once, twice.

After a while, the daughter lets go of the seat belt. A red welt crosses her palm. She opens the door. The scent of moss and fresh buds seeps into the car. Birds chirp, and the nearby spring tinkles its quiet silver laughter. The hot engine settles with pings.

Mother and daughter fill the canisters. It hasn't rained for a long time, and the flow of the spring is weak. The mother carries four canisters at a time back to the car. The water sloshes behind milky plastic. When they are done, she opens the door of their car and, one hand atop the door, the other on her hip, says, "Come!" Her cheekbones reflect the sun.

Martina pulls her fingertips out of the cool stream and walks around the car. She puts on her seat belt. The sound of the engine starting blocks out the birds and the mountain stream. Her mother's knuckles rest on the steering wheel, solid, symmetrical. As they zigzag their way down, the girl waits for the yell "Jump!" to erupt from her mother. She waits for the wheels to lose traction. She imagines the switch-backs leading back and forth, back and forth, and wonders whether, over the many days of water fetching, a direction will emerge from this, a road forward, an escape. She cups the seat belt buckle with her hand. She's prepared.

Barnes

Edmundo Paz Soldán

I T WAS ALL a mistake, Barnes understood, locked in his jail cell. He would proudly stick to the truth. Later, however, in a dim room, blinding light in his eyes, the interrogation began, accusations about assassinating the president, and he pondered his mediocrity, the massive insignificance of his life—and feeling the vain, useless weight of importance for the first time, said, yes, he had indeed killed the president. Whereupon he was accused of planting the bomb that killed two hundred eighty-seven soldiers in Tarapacá's regiment; all he could do was laugh with contempt, embracing the blame. Later, he confessed without pause to sabotaging the gas line, which left Bolivia wrecked economically, to having started the fire consuming ninety-two percent of Cochabamba's forested parks; to exploding the four LAB jets mid-flight, and raping the daughter of La Paz's North American ambassador. They would execute him by firing squad at sunrise the next day, they announced. Indeed they should do so: a man like him, he agreed, had no right to live.

Translated by Kirk Nesset

A Sailor

Randa Jarrar

SHE FUCKS A sailor, a Turkish sailor, the summer she spends in Istanbul. When she comes home to Wisconsin, it takes her three days to come clean about it to her husband.

He says this doesn't bother him, and she tells him that it bothers her that it doesn't bother him. He asks if she prefers him to be the kind of man who is bothered by fleeting moments, and she tells him that yes, she prefers that he be that kind of man. He tells her he thinks she married him because he is precisely the kind of man who doesn't dwell on fleeting moments, because he is the kind of man who does not hold a grudge. She tells him that holding a grudge and working up some anger about one's wife fucking a sailor is not the same thing. He agrees that holding a grudge isn't the same as working up some anger about one's wife fucking a sailor, but, he adds, one's wife, specifically his own, would never leave him for a sailor, and not a Turkish sailor. In fact, he says, she did not leave him for the Turkish sailor. She is here. So why should he be angry?

Now, she becomes angry, and asks him why he assumes she did not consider leaving him for the sailor. Besides, she says, she and the sailor shared a Muslim cultural identity, something she does not share with her husband. She asks him if he thought of that.

He says he had not thought of it, and that even if she had considered leaving him for the Turkish sailor, she must have decided not to. And he acquiesces that the Turkish sailor and she must have shared a strong bond over being culturally Muslim, because, he says, he cannot imagine what else she would have had in common with a Turkish sailor.

Plenty! she shouts at him. She had plenty in common with the Turkish sailor.

Her husband wants to know what she had in common with the Turkish sailor.

She had nothing in common with the Turkish sailor except that she was attracted to him and he was attracted to her and they spent a night in an unairconditioned room in Karakoy, by Galata tower. In the morning, she woke up to the sound of seagulls circling the tower, zooming around it hungrily, loudly. The Turkish sailor had heard the seagulls too. Then, she had left. That was really all they had in common: the cultural identity, the sex, and the seagulls.

She tells her husband this story. He asks her what she wants him to say. She tells him to say that he is angry that she fucked a Turkish sailor. She tells him to say that he wishes he had fucked her in the unairconditioned room near Galata tower. She tells him to shout it.

Her husband refuses to say any of it. His refusal is quiet, itself not angry.

When she sees him placidly gazing at her, and refusing to say any of these things, she understands that this is his way of getting back at her for fucking the Turkish sailor.

And she also understand that this, his lack of passion, his sense of logic, is one of the reasons she fucked the Turkish sailor, and, it is also the reason she came home.

The Voice of the Enemy

Juan Villoro

WHEN MEXICO CITY still existed I wore a beautiful yellow helmet. I listened to telephone conversations on top of a pole. The sky was a morning of cables; the electricity vibrated, wrapped in soft plastics. From time to time a thick blue spark fell to the street. That moment justified my being on the pole. My belt was filled with tools but I preferred a small pair of bird-beak pliers. Their bite mended the wound, the electricity ran again.

In front, there was a movie theater with a cardboard castle rising above the marquee. In back, a building was switching on red lights to protect it from planes. Their engines were making a noise, but it was impossible to see them in the thick sky.

The Electrical Supervisor demanded that we keep a close ear on the cables. Our enemies were making their way to us. I didn't know who they were, but I knew they were coming: it was necessary to listen to calls, to search for anything strange in them. One raining afternoon, tied to the pole, I heard a strange voice. The woman was talking as if she were trying to hide; in a soft tone, frightened, she said "birdseed," "brightness," "magnolia," "broken balcony." I was there to listen to conversations and guarantee that they flowed without interruptions. I heard those random words, vibrating like a senseless code. I was supposed to report them, but I didn't do anything; I allowed someone else, somewhere else, to understand what I didn't understand.

A few days later I found out about the scorched palm trees. The enemies burned a neighborhood where there were still plants. Fixed to my pole, I couldn't tell if the city was expanding or shrinking. Occasionally, between trumpets and bugles, loyal troops would talk on the cables; then a bomb, the grating voice of another militia.

On the opposite corner something strange happened; the yellow helmet didn't move for several hours. I tried to let someone know that my coworker was dead; my fingers bled dialing so many busy numbers. As I looked at the motionless helmet, I heard the soft, terrifying words again: "bedroom," "cinnamon," "statue." I imagined, thoroughly envious, that those words were a message for someone else. For me they were just sad. I didn't talk to the Electrical Supervisor then either.

Early one morning an explosion shook me. I opened the wiring box: the photoelectric sensors were emitting a putrid smoke. I turned on my flashlight; I had batteries to last for weeks but something told me that the pole wouldn't last that long.

During his calls, the Supervisor said: "Whoever controls the cables controls the city." The enemies had cut the electricity, the movie theater burned in a reddish cloud, but the phones were working. I heard the woman say "fragrance," "planets," "candy," "smooth stones." I couldn't report her. Slowly, terrified, and with precise cruelty, I understood how wonderful the enemy's voice was.

I must have been asleep when they took my coworker

down from the opposite post. It was my turn next; a gloved hand pulled me by my back. I was drunk from breathing the malignant air, and I never found out how I left the burning city.

For weeks, perhaps months, I've been living in a room with metal walls. They showed me a terrible photo on a computer. It's called *City of Palaces* and it shows the movie theater with its cardboard castle, the tall building in the back, and the cables that I once took care of. "There's sixty-seven," said the voice of my captor. It was true. I was in charge of sixty-seven cables and I protected them from our imprecise enemies. For days that were indistinguishable from night I saved the electricity and the calls. Only once did I damage a cable. It happened a few days before I came down from the pole.

The only thing left of the city is photographs. If I pointed out the damaged cable, my guards would be able to enter the labyrinth, follow the thread to the photograph, to the house where that different voice lived. In front of me are the sixty-seven cables that were my life. One of them can take them to the woman. I know which one. But I'm not going to say.

Translated by George Henson

An Imperial Message

Franz Kafka

THE EMPEROR HAS sent a message, directly from his death-bed, to you alone, his pathetic subject, a tiny shadow which has taken refuge at the furthest distance from the imperial sun. He ordered the herald to kneel down beside his bed and whispered the message in his ear. He thought it was so important that he had the herald speak it back to him. He confirmed the accuracy of the verbal message by nodding his head. And in front of the entire crowd of those witnessing his death—all the obstructing walls have been broken down, and all the great ones of his empire are standing in a circle on the broad and high soaring flights of stairs—in front of all of them he dispatched his herald. The messenger started off at once, a powerful, tire-less man. Sticking one arm out and then another, he makes his way through the crowd. If he runs into resistance, he points to his breast where there is a sign of the sun. So he moves forward easily, unlike anyone else. But the crowd is so huge; its dwelling places are infinite. If there were an open field, how he would fly along, and soon you would hear the marvelous pounding of his fist on your door. But instead of that, how futile are all his efforts. He is still forcing his way through the private rooms of the innermost palace. Never will he win his way through. And if he did manage that, nothing would have been achieved. He would have to fight his way down the steps, and, if he managed to do that, nothing would have been achieved. He would have to stride through the courtyards, and after the courtyards through the second palace encircling the first, and, then again, through stairs and courtyards, and then, once again, a palace, and so on for thousands of years. And if he finally burst through the outermost door—but that can never, never happen—the royal capital city, the center of the world, is still there in front of him, piled high and full of sediment. No one pushes his way through here, certainly not someone with a message from a dead man. But you sit at your window and dream of that message when evening comes.

Translated by Ian Johnston

Trilogy

Antonio López Ortega

HAVE THREE SONS by three different men. The first was a Kurd in the resistance living in exile in Paris; the second was a Belgian from Antwerp, a functionary in his country's embassy; the third was a Chilean painter who had his studio in the Place d'Italie. I had relationships with all three while I was still a young student in France.

I have raised my sons with passion. Since my return to Caracas, my mother has had to make space for me in her house in San Bernardino. The boys run around and play in the garden. They are three brothers with three different last names; there have been certain difficulties when it was time to enroll them in school.

Each one inherited a different trait from his father: the oldest, the green eyes and height of the Kurd; the middle one, the straight hair and the indifference of the Belgian; the third, the distant self-absorption of the Chilean. I like this variety, this symphony. It's like having my past fresh, running around the house; it's like having all the variety concentrated in one place.

Strengths and weaknesses accompany me; also the good and the bad moments. Some days are happy (the birthdays, the day trips) and others truly wretched (the recurrent nightmares of the littlest one). The boys develop without ghosts and I have tried to make paternity a remote idea compared to my mother's warm house.

I see each one's face and I think I am seeing each of their fathers. They are interwoven sequels: the encounters in the cafés, the parties, the parks, the trips to the movies, the museums. They were distinct worlds: from the lurking danger of the Kurd (a true paranoid who couldn't meet me in a café without constantly looking in every direction), passing through the Belgian's diplomatic coolness, ending in the Chilean's romantic passion, always jumping from his canvases to my body or vice versa. All of that richness runs through me from head to tail and, upon remembering, I tremble, I long for the past.

My sons have grown up without any great traumas and I can say that now they are young men. What a shame that with such a great variety no man wants me now. Occasionally I go out on a date with one or another but I have learned to omit any reference to my sons. Each day the boys spend more time with my mother and less time with me. I know that they'll be fine at home. Taking them anywhere is a problem in the agitated life of these times. I have begun to travel with a few friends, I have met other men. Only this time I have taken care not to leave any traces.

Translated by Nathan Budoff

Shattered

Shirani Rajapakse

S HE WAS WALKING down the road minding her own business when the sound exploded in front of her. It shattered the sound barrier and sent off sparks in all directions. She stopped in her tracks; there was nowhere to go. Her feet flew in the air and her hair touched the pavement. Lightning flashed all around her. Thunder roared inside her head. Her left eardrum beat a series of staccatos and strained to pop out as the thunder roared its way down her ears. From the corner of her eye she faintly saw the eardrum roll away along the pavement as if in a hurry to get someplace, any place, other than her loud resonating ear.

Nidisha knew she had fallen to the ground as someone trampled on her hand in a hurry to get to somewhere else. She didn't see who it was for the brightness of the sun overhead and the million and one flashing lights in her eyes; blue, red, yellow and green like the brightly colored lights hung in homes and along roads during Vesak. Nidisha tried to call out but the road to her voice was cut open and lay gasping on the ground next to her. She couldn't hear, she couldn't see, she couldn't speak. She was like the three wise monkeys all rolled into one. What happened?

She couldn't move either. Nidisha felt herself lying across the pavement that not so long ago held her feet upright. She could feel something but wasn't quite sure what it was she felt. Was it her arm lying by her side, the one trampled on? And was that her leg jutting out in an ungainly manner? What was it? she wondered. It was then that it struck her that she was no longer there.

Someone had taken away her right to walk on the road. That someone had strapped bombs to her breasts and exploded herself not so far away. That was the loud noise Nidisha heard, louder than thunder, that shattered her a few minutes ago. She was no longer there. Yet Nidisha still felt herself moving, willing herself to walk to where she was supposed to go. But how, and where?

She felt warmth flowing around her. Puddles were collecting but there was no rain. The bright sun glared at her through the ugly grey smoke swirling, swirling around. The puddles became a small pond and then took on the shape of a stream. It began to flow, flow toward the ocean five miles away. Her juices were flowing out fast and furious down the pavement and all over the road. Very soon it would reach the ocean, of that she was certain. She flowed and as she did others joined her on her way. Tiny streams seeking answers, they flowed in the same direction. They turned into a river. They flowed into the sea waiting to take them in.

And all around her people were screaming their heads off. At least those that still had them on. She couldn't see, could barely hear but she could sense it all. They had all dropped like flies and there were more to come. And it all happened because she had dared to defy the terrorists and go to work that day. But what was so wrong with that?

Bruise

Stuart Dybek

SHE CAME OVER wearing a man's white shirt, rolled up at the sleeves, and a faded blue denim jumper that made her eyes appear even more blue.

"Look," she said, sitting down on the couch and slowly raising the jumper up her legs, revealing a bruise high on the outside of her thigh.

It was summer. Bearded painters in spattered coveralls were painting the outside of the house white. Through the open windows they could hear the painters scraping the old, flaking paint from the siding on one side of the house, and the slap of paint-soaked brushes from the other.

"These old boards really suck up the paint," one of the painters would remark from time to time.

"I've always bruised so easily," she said, lowering her voice as if the painters might hear.

The bruise looked blue behind the tan mesh of nylon. It was just off the hip and above it he could see the black, lacy band of her panties. It was a hot day, climbing toward ninety, and as he studied the spot that she held her dress up for him to see, it occurred to him that even now, at this moment, there was a choice. Things between them might not be as irrevocable as they seemed. It occurred to him suddenly as he studied the bruise that it still might be possible to say something between them that wasn't charged with secret meanings. The direction their lives were uncontrollably taking might be changed, not by some revelation, but in the course of an ordinary conversation, by the twist of a wisecrack, or a joke, or perhaps by a simple question. He might ask why she was wearing panty hose on such a hot day. Was it that her legs weren't tanned yet? He might rise from the couch and ask her if she would like a lemonade, and when she said yes, he would go to the kitchen and make it—real lemonade squeezed from the lemons in his refrigerator, their cold juice stirred with sugar and water, the granulated sugar whispering amidst the ice, the ice cubes in a sweating glass pitcher clunking like a temple bell.

They could sit, sipping from cool glasses and talking about something as uncomplicated as weather, gabbing in the easy way of painters, not because they lacked for more interesting things to talk about, but because it was summer and hot and she seemed not to have noticed the heat.

Instead, when she crossed her legs in a way that hiked her dress higher and moved her body toward him, he touched the bruise with his fingertip, and pressed it more softly than one presses an elevator button.

"Oh," her lips formed, though she didn't quite say it. She exhaled, closing her blue eyes, then opening them wider, almost in surprise, and stared at him. They were sitting very close together, their faces almost touching.

When he took his finger away she stretched the nylon over the bruise so he could more clearly see its different gradations of blue. A pale, green sheen surrounded it like an aura; purple capillaries ran off in all directions like tiny cracks, like a network of rivers on a map; there was violet at its center like a stain.

"It's ugly isn't it," she asked in a whisper.

He didn't answer, but pressed it again, slowly, deeply, and her head tilted back against a cushion. This time the oh of her lips was audible. She closed her eyes and moaned, uncrossing her legs and running her fingernails up the insides of her thighs. They were sitting so close together that the sound of her nails scraping along nylon seemed to him almost a clatter the painters would hear. Her legs spread and he cupped his hand over her lap and felt the cushion of hair through the nylon, and heat, actual heat, like summer through a screen door, reflecting off his palm.

He pressed the bruise again and again. Each time she reshaped her lips into a vowel that sounded increasingly surprised.

Outside, the house turned progressively whiter. The summer sun dissolved into golden, vaporish rays in the trees. The bruise—he never asked how she got it—spread across the sky.

Love

Edgar Omar Avilés

"I'M SURE NOW, Mommy," the girl said to her mother, breaking into tears. "God is really there, and he's full of love!"

"Why are you so sure?"

"I've seen him and he spoke to me from heaven. It's the most wonderful place in the world!" The girl answered so assuredly and fervently that all her mother could do was to stab her with the knife she was chopping an onion with.

The girl was so young, still without sin. Her life was so miserable, she begged for change on the streets. Surely, in no time she would start selling her body. Then the glorious heaven and her God full of love would no longer accept her.

For her part she would go to hell, the mother thought while driving the knife in for the tenth time.

Translated by Toshiya Kamei

First Impressions

Ricardo Sumalavia

I N THE MONTHS before the end of my last year of high school, I began working in the afternoons at a small printing press. My mother was not opposed. I was friendly with the owner as well as his wife, an enormous and attractive woman who visited my house now and then so my mother could cut her hair or dye it in whatever color current style demanded. I learned the publishing trade with the enthusiasm of one who hoped to see his own poems in print one day. For the time being, I was only in charge of placing letters of lead type, and I was always careful not to get them out of order, so that I wouldn't have to place them all again, line by line, as tended to happen whenever Señora Leonor, the owner's wife, came by the print shop. Her presence was always a bit unsettling to me, and she was well aware of this. I suspect she had always known it, even before I did, ever since I was a child, when I didn't understand the transitory pleasure that came from brushing against her legs or her hips on the pretext of playing with my little cars, before I was sent out to the patio, leaving Señora Leonor and that smile that would electrify me years later in her husband's print shop. If her visits were sporadic, it only made the effect more disconcerting: an unease that I tried to pour into my adolescent poems, to be transferred later onto an old plank of wood in the composition box that I kept hidden beneath the other work of the day—that is, if my shame didn't force me to undo it all.

In this way the months passed, and, with the end of the year, my schooling, too, came to a close. It was natural, then, that the print shop should become my full-time job, at a higher salary and with all the respect accorded an adult employee—or so the owner informed me in early January. His wife, with short, red hair and a miniskirt of the kind worn at the end of the sixties—justified by the intense heat of that summer—came to visit more and more often. I should confess that the color of her hair, contrasted with her pale skin, inspired what I considered to be my best poem. And the longest. The only one I was, without misgivings, able to set in type, and the only one I was prepared to show to its muse. Of course, I imagined a thousand ways of offering her the poem, certain that her only response would be to keep me in suspense with a kiss on the cheek perhaps, or with the touch of her fingernail along my chin.

Until the appropriate afternoon came. It was a Thursday, the day of her usual visits, and her husband had gone out to pick up a few rolls of paper. I had used the opportunity to typeset and ink my poem when Señora Leonor appeared, red-haired and wearing a miniskirt, intensely pale in spite of the summer sun. I don't recall exactly what she said, I only know that she ordered me to close the door of the shop, and then called me to the back. She stood before me, contemplating me for a moment, with a hint of that smile I knew so well, and then she kissed me. She used her hands to

guide mine, so that I might caress her body, lift her miniskirt easily, and drop her underwear, which may or not have
been fashionable in those days but which shook me the very
moment I saw it. In this state of intoxication I pushed her to
the worktable, where I leaned her back and climbed on top
of her, on top of the impressive Señora Leonor, who received
me with moans and tremors of excitement.

We stayed that way for a long while, until satisfaction
and good sense separated us. It was when she got up from
the table that I discovered, perplexed, the fate of my poem.
It was printed on the woman's back. In truth, the opening, which was on her lumbar region, could be read very
clearly, while the final verses, which spread to her expan-
sive ass, were blurry, nothing more than senseless marks of
ink. Though I've tried to explain it to myself, I still can't
quite understand my silence. I let her get dressed, let her bid
me farewell with an affectionate kiss. It was the only time I
managed to reshuffle the lead type on the plank that had held
my poem. I could reshuffle others, I told myself, in the free
moments of some future employment.

Translated by Daniel Alarcón

Fire. Water.

Avital Gad-Cykman

THE SON FLIES an airplane over the handrail. The daughter yells she won't wash her hair. The son throws a bomb at her, into the living room. The daughter looks for the electric heater. The mother washes the dishes. The father walks the dog outside.

The son rides the mezzanine's half wall. The daughter says she will die, because the day is too cold for a shower. The son, he slips down the handrail, a small skate in his hands. The daughter, she carries the heater to the bathroom. The son piles blankets by the bathroom to build a barricade. The mother washes dishes in the kitchen. The father walks the dog outside.

The son kicks the bathroom door open. The daughter screams she is cold. The son sends the skate into the bathroom. The daughter drags one blanket inside. The son looks at the bathroom mirror. The daughter is naked. The son laughs out loud. The mother washes dishes. The father walks the dog outside.

The daughter shouts she'll show around the picture with

the son's butt out. The son dives onto the floor for his skate and his jet. The daughter cries he should not see her. The son turns on the water to fly his jet through waterfalls. The daughter shows the finger to the son. The son throws his skate at the daughter. The daughter shouts, "Mother! Father!" The mother washes dishes. The father walks the dog outside.

The son jumps up and down like a monkey. The daughter leaps at the son. The son bumps into the electric heater, and he and the heater fall down. The daughter throws the blanket at him. The son gets up and covers her head with the blanket. The daughter says she is warm and good. The son pushes the daughter at the water. The daughter falls over the heater with the blanket over her head. The son drops the jet, the bombs, the skate and pulls her from the heater. The blanket's hem turns black. The mother washes the dishes. The father walks the dog outside.

The daughter falls. The son pulls. The daughter rises. Falls, Rises. Throws. Pulls. The son. The daughter. The electric heater. The water in the shower. Fire. Water. The mother washes the dishes. The father walks the dog outside.

KENYA

The Snake

Eric Rugara

THE KID SAW it first. Everyone else was busy talking and
sipping tea when the kid suddenly cried out, "Snake!"
The father leapt up, swift, like a Maasai Moran. "Where?"
"There!" At the end of the kid's pointed finger was the gray
wall and on the gray wall, above the window and next to
the door was a long, black thing slithering. Against the wall
was a table the father leapt upon with all the young blood
pounding in his veins. "Get me a big stick!" he yelled. The
mother was out and back in a second holding a long wooden
pole and handed it to the father and all the hidden talent for
warfare that the father had came out in the open when he
handled that pole with utmost skill and a surprising dexter-
ity, driving it into the head of the snake as though it was a
part of his arms, like throwing a punch, and the snake fell
off the wall and onto the floor and the father jumped off
the table and pushed out the snake with the opposite end
of the pole and someone said, "Watch out!" but the father
was fast and he leapt back as the snake's head lashed at him
and he brought down the pole on the snake's head and he

pushed it out with all his might and it soared through the air, out the door, and onto the ground, raising a small cloud of dust. "Make sure it doesn't get onto the grass," someone said. "Once it gets on the grass you won't see it, it will zip off like a flash of lightning." But the father was somewhere else: in the zone he raised the pole, with both hands, over his head and commenced to bring it down upon the body and head and tail of the snake even as it tried to lash back, beat it mercilessly till it was battered and dead and the skin peeled off in certain places, beat it till its head was like chewed-up meat. "Let's burn it," he said. The mother went back in and came out with a can of oil and a red lighter, the father handled the snake on the opposite end of the pole and everyone followed him to the rubbish pit where the oil was poured on it and the fire caught upon it and its snake skin came alive and twisted and coiled as it broiled and burned and everyone felt very, very good especially the father and the kid who were the heroes of the moment, the kid for his keen eyes, the father for his leap into action and his brilliance with the pole and everyone trooped back into the house and a fresh thermos of tea was brought in and everyone poured it into their cups and chattered about the moment, the emotion, the action and the aliveness that they felt.

An Ugly Man

Marcela Fuentes

O N HER LUNCH break, she dumps Luis for Daniel Towens, the ugliest man in the county.

She and Luis meet at the downtown café Luis hates. He picks a table next to the window to keep an eye on the parking meter. There's an old beater truck in the space he wanted and he grumbles that the guy is probably not even a customer. Nothing but hipsters eat here, he says, artsy gringos and uppity high-spanics like her, who like to spend money when they can make a fucking sandwich at home. He scowls out the café window.

Daniel Towens steps out of the credit union across the street. He stands on the sidewalk waiting for the traffic to clear. Daniel is lanky and mercilessly freckled. He wears dusty green coveralls with National Park Service stitched on the pocket. He has an unfortunate arrangement of teeth. They jut from his mouth like fossilized woodchips.

Fuck that's an ugly guero, Luis says. He thinks it's funny that Daniel is sweet on her. When she frowns Luis flashes a shark grin, all razor and gleam. Fuckin' ugly, he says again, and bites his roast beef sandwich.

She doesn't tell Luis not to be rude. She purses her mouth around her straw and sucks cold lemon water. She pretends she's not listening, although the couple at a nearby table shift to look at him. Her face stiffens with the effort of indifference, lacquers over, smooth as riverbed sand.

In the desert, Daniel glides over rocky caliche and scrub brush. He leads hikers and artists and anthropologists on expeditions through the chaparral, identifying varieties of lichens and cacti, spelunking for prehistoric rock art. But he crosses the street with his face to the ground, hunching his chicken-thin shoulders, a hank of dull hair splayed on his green collar.

He stops, his back to the café window, and digs in his front pocket. The small truck, white and latticed with dried mud, appears to be his. Luis knocks on the glass and waves. Daniel squints. He offers an uncertain closed-lipped smile.

You're funny, she says, standing up. She walks out of the café. Luis says hey-hey-hey, the word tugged out of him in sharp little jerks.

Daniel, she says. She steps into him, so close his head blocks the hard afternoon light. He smells like bluff sage and wind. His eyes are mild as cloud shadows. She sets her mouth on the wilderness of his mouth, lets it open against the rough structures of his teeth.

The Lord of the Flies

Marco Denevi

THE FLIES IMAGINED their god. It was also a fly. The lord of the flies was a fly, now green, now black and gold, now pink, now white, now purple, an inconceivable fly, a beautiful fly, a monstrous fly, a terrible fly, a benevolent fly, a vengeful fly, a just fly, a youthful fly, but always a fly. Some embellished his size so that he was compared to an ox, others imagined him to be so small that you couldn't see him. In some religions, he was missing wings ("He flies," they argued, "but he doesn't need wings"), while in others he had infinite wings. Here it was said he had antennae like horns, and there that he had eyes that surrounded his entire head. For some he buzzed constantly, and for others he was mute, but he could communicate just the same. And for everyone, when flies died, he took them up to paradise. Paradise was a hunk of rotten meat, stinking and putrid, that souls of the dead flies could gnaw on for an eternity without devouring it; yes, this heavenly scrap of refuse would be constantly reborn and regenerated under the swarm of flies. For the good flies. Because there were also bad flies, and for them there was a hell. The hell for condemned flies was a place without excrement, without waste, trash, stink, without anything of anything; a place sparkling with cleanliness and illuminated by a bright white light; in other words, an ungodly place.

Translated by José Chaves

Honor Killing

Kim Young-ha

S HE WAS TWENTY-ONE, with fair, beautiful skin. Even
when bare, her face glowed, always radiant and dewy.
This was precisely why the dermatologist's office hired her
as the receptionist. Her job was simple. All she had to do was
write down the patients' names, tell them in a friendly voice,
"Please take a seat until we call your name," find their charts,
and hand them over to the nurses. Her glowing, translucent
skin created high expectations, encouraging the patients to
place their trust in the office, which bustled with a sudden
increase in patients.

But one day, her face started to break out. The problem began with the appearance of a small pimple, growing worse and worse until it spread across her entire face.
Nobody could figure out why. At first, the young doctor,
who had only managed to start the business with the help of
bank loans, treated her lightheartedly, but later zeroed in on
her with desperation. And the more he focused on her, the
more her condition worsened. Red spots covered her face,
making her look like a splotchy pizza from far away. The

despondent doctor pulled out his hair and the nurses hated her. One spring day, she left behind a note—"I apologize to everyone. I'm sorry"—and committed suicide. The office hired a new receptionist. Her skin was so luminous that it forced everyone's eyes shut.

Translated by Chi-Young Kim

Signs

Bess Winter

I T IS AFTER a series of nubile young researchers have begun to parade through Koko the gorilla's life that she learns the sign for *nipple*. She draws her heavy arms close to her chest, and her leathery pointers spring out toward the unsuspecting graduate student. A look of expectation settles onto her simian face. Sometimes her gaze rests on the soft-sloping clavicle that betrays itself from beneath an unbuttoned collar, sometimes on the ponytail that rests coyly on one shoulder like a thick tassel, and sometimes on the face of Dr. Thomas, senior supervising researcher, as if she's asking him whether she's doing it right.

Inevitably, the student looks to Dr. Thomas. *What should I do? What should I say?*

Nipple, signs Koko.

Inevitably, Dr. Thomas tells her it is her duty, as a paid researcher, not to interfere: that she should indulge Koko's fetish, that this, too, should be researched.

Inevitably, there is a long moment while the student struggles with the request. Dr. Thomas fumbles his pencil, tapping it against his notepad, twirling it between two fingers. He does this until the student takes in a long, reedy breath, looks down to unbutton her blouse with shaking hands.

Then there is the moment when she peels off her blouse and unhooks her bra, and the moment when she sets the bra beside her on the table or hangs it by one strap over the edge of the chair.

Dr. Thomas knows there are two types of graduate students: the ones who put their bras beside them on the table and the ones who hang them behind themselves on the chair. They may be further categorized by type of bra: underwire, sports. Then there are those who don't wear bras at all. He can never predict which students will not be wearing bras, except that these young women are usually small-breasted, gamine.

And there is the inscrutable moment between woman and beast when the researcher, breathing fast, sits half-clad in front of the gorilla, and the gorilla does not sign at all. When the researcher tries to avoid a direct gaze into the gorilla's eyes lest she provoke her, she cannot; Koko seems to address her directly and without words. Dr. Thomas jots down notes, but he cannot understand why, in this moment, Koko reaches out to take the students' hands. He can only hypothesize about why some graduate students cry at the slightest touch and why some smile at the gorilla, why some curl into Koko's arms when she opens them. Why some allow her to touch and gentle them, to trace their eyes and nose and soft neck with her rough fingers. Why some nod knowingly, and why the gorilla nods back, and why he feels a sudden shift in the room, as if he's the unwelcome guest at a sacred rite.

He can only guess at this, too: why, after each student leaves for the day, and it's just Dr. Thomas and Koko, the gorilla regards him with a withering look. Why she pokes at her fruit and then looks up at him like a wife waiting to broach a touchy topic at dinner.

And why, when she finally signs to him, *nipple*, he searches her earth-brown eyes for some silent instruction. But if there are words in those eyes, he can't find them. Those eyes are deep and ripe. They're unmapped territory. He doesn't know whether to remove his shirt or call back a graduate student. With a shy hand, he touches his collar and makes to open it. But before he completes the gesture the moment passes, or he has done the wrong thing already. Koko looks away.

Idolatry

Sherman Alexie

MARIE WAITED FOR hours. That was okay. She was Indian and everything Indian—powwows, funerals, and weddings—required patience. This audition wasn't Indian, but she was ready when they called her name.

"What are you going to sing?" the British man asked.

"Patsy Cline," she said.

"Let's hear it."

She'd only sung the first verse before he stopped her.

"You are a terrible singer," he said. "Never sing again."

She knew this moment would be broadcast on national television. She'd already agreed to accept any humiliation.

"But my friends, my voice coaches, *my mother*, they all say I'm great."

"They lied."

How many songs had Marie sung in her life? How many lies had she been told? On camera, Marie did the cruel math, rushed into the green room, and wept in her mother's arms.

In this world, we must love the liars or go unloved.

Lost

Alberto Fuguet

N A COUNTRY filled with missing people, disappearing is easy. All the efforts are concentrated on the dead, so those of us who are among the living can fade quickly away. They won't come looking; they won't even realize you're gone. If I've seen you before, I don't remember. You see, everyone down there has bad memories. Either they don't remember, or they simply don't want to.

A professor once told me that I was lost. I replied that in order to lose yourself, first you'd have to know where you are.

Then I thought, *What if it's the reverse?*

I was erased for fifteen years. I abandoned everything, including myself. There was a quiz I never took. My girl-friend was having a birthday party and I never showed up. I got on a bus bound for Los Vilos. I didn't have a plan; it just happened. It was what had to happen, and there was no turning back.

At first I felt guilty. Then pursued. Would they be after me? Would they find me? What if I run into someone?

But I didn't run into anybody.

They say that the world is a handkerchief. It's not. People who say that don't know what the world is like. It's huge and—above all—strange and foreign. You can roam far and wide and nobody will care.

Now I'm an adult. In some ways. I've got hair on my back, and sometimes the zipper doesn't zip. I've been to a lot of places and done things I never thought I'd do. But you survive. You get used to things. Nothing is so bad. Nothing.

I've been to a lot of places. Have you been to Tumbes? To the port of Buenaventura? Or San Pedro Sula? How about Memphis?

Like a puppy, I followed a Kmart checkout girl as far as El Centro, California, a town that smelled of fertilizer. The relationship started off better than it ended. Then I went to work in the casinos in Laughlin, Nevada, that lined the Colorado River. I lived in a house across the way from Bullhead City with a woman named Frances and a guy named Frank, but we never saw each other. We left each other notes. Both of them were bad spellers.

Once, in a diner in Tulsa, a woman told me that I reminded her of a son who'd never come home. "Why do you think he left?" she asked. I said I didn't know. But maybe I did.

Or maybe not.

Without wanting to, I ended up teaching English to Hispanic kids in Galveston. The Texas flag looks a lot like Chile's. One of the girls died in my arms. She fell off the swing set: I'd pushed too hard and she flew out of the seat. It seemed like she flew for two minutes through the hazy Gulf sky. I didn't want to hurt her, but nevertheless, I did. So . . . what?

What can you do?

Have you been to Mérida, on the Yucatán? In the summer there it hits 108 degrees, and they close off the downtown area on Sundays so the people can dance. Sometimes I find a girl and join in.

Last year I decided to Google my own name. Maybe they were searching for me. But even I couldn't find myself. Just a guy with the same name as me who lives in "Barquisimeto, Venezuela," and has a dental practice. He has three children and believes in God.

Sometimes I dream about living in Barquisimeto, having three children, and believing in God. Sometimes, I even dream that they have found me.

Translated by Ezra E. Fitz

The Extravagant Behavior of the Naked Woman

Josefina Estrada

THE WOMAN WHO walks naked through the streets of Santa María provokes astonishment in the children, delight in the men, and incredulity and anger in the women. She sits down at the corner of Sor Juana Inés de la Cruz and Sabino, next to the bicycle repair shop. The children come out of the two adjacent slums and cross the street to watch her as she sniffs glue from a bag, her only possession. She doesn't seem to care that she's naked, yet neither could you say that she'd made a conscious decision to display her dark, abundant flesh.

Even when she's sitting down you can tell she's a woman of vast stature. At shoulder level, her hair is a mass of tangles that contains balls of chewing gum, bits of earth, dust and fluff. The applause and whistles of the onlookers grow louder when she opens her legs and begins to scratch herself hard in the most impenetrable part of her being. At this point, the young men, who are always hanging around, can't suppress their laughter. Instinctively, as if fearing that at any moment they too might reveal their mysteries, they finger the flies of their trousers.

And when the woman lies down and turns her back on them, the onlookers begin throwing things at her. She takes a while to react, but they all know that as soon as she sits up, she'll get to her feet and chase her attackers. And the children will then be able to see that her breasts are not, in fact, stuck fast to her ample abdomen. Some of the smaller children go and tell their mothers that "the woman who wears no underpants or anything" is on the loose again. And their mothers forbid them to go back outside.

There was a period when she was seen by several women near where Aldama crosses Mina. Then for two years she prowled up and down Avenida Guerrero. She would go to sleep surrounded by a pile of clothes donated by well-meaning people, and which served as both pillow and mattress. When she grew tired of her bundle of clothes, she would burn it using the same solvent she inhaled.

The huge, dark woman goes into building sites to wash. The glee of the workers reaches its height when she bends over to drink from the tap. They're beside themselves with excitement when she picks up handfuls of lime and powders her armpits. Any man bold enough to approach her has always been repelled by the ferocity of her insults. The women who live around Calle Sor Juana complain not about the exhibition she makes of herself but about the fact that she's freer than the men. Instead of putting an end to the extravagant behavior of this woman—which arouses lewd thoughts even in the most saintly of men—the police, they say, spend all their time arresting drunks.

Translated by Margaret Jull Costa

Sleeping Habit

Yasunari Kawabata

STARTLED BY A sharp pain, as if her hair were being pulled out, she woke up three or four times. But when she realized that a skein of her black hair was wound around the neck of her lover, she smiled to herself. In the morning, she would say, "My hair is this long now. When we sleep together, it truly grows longer."

Quietly, she closed her eyes.

"I don't want to sleep. Why do we have to sleep? Even though we are lovers, to have to go to sleep, of all things!" On nights when it was all right for her to stay with him, she would say this, as if it were a mystery to her.

"You'd have to say that people make love precisely because they have to sleep. A love that never sleeps—the very idea is frightening. It's something thought up by a demon."

"That's not true. At first, we neither slept either, did we? There's nothing so selfish as sleep."

That was the truth. As soon as he fell asleep, he would pull his arm out from under her neck, frowning unconsciously as he did so. She, too, no matter where she embraced him, would find when she awakened that the strength had gone out of her arm.

"Well, then, I'll wind my hair around and around your arm and hold you tight."

Winding the sleeve of his sleeping kimono around her arm, she'd held him hard. Just the same, sleep stole away the strength from her fingers.

"All right, then, just as the old proverb says, I'll tie you up with the rope of a woman's hair." So saying, she'd drawn a long skein of her raven-black hair around his neck.

That morning, however, he smiled at what she said.

"What do you mean, your hair has grown longer? It's so tangled up you can't pass a comb through it."

As time went by, they forgot about that sort of thing. These nights, she slept as if she'd even forgotten he was there. But, if she happened to wake up, her arm was always touching him—and his arm was touching her. By now, when they no longer thought about it, it had become their sleeping habit.

Translated by Lane Dunlop

Night Drive

Rubem Fonseca

ARRIVED HOME WITH my briefcase bulging with papers, reports, studies, research, proposals, contracts. My wife, who was playing solitaire in bed, a glass of whiskey on the nightstand, said, without glancing up from the cards, "You look tired." The usual house sounds: my daughter in her room practicing voice modulation, quadraphonic music from my son's room. "Why don't you put down that suitcase?" my wife asked. "Take off those clothes, have a nice glass of whiskey. You've got to learn to relax."

I went to the library, the place in the house where I enjoy being by myself, and, as usual, did nothing. I opened the research volume on the desk but didn't see the letters and numbers. I was merely waiting. "You never stop working. I'll bet your partners don't work half as hard and they earn the same." My wife came into the room, a glass in her hand. "Can I tell her to serve dinner?"

The maid served the meal French style. My children had grown up; my wife and I were fat. "It's that wine you like," she said, clicking her tongue with pleasure. My son asked for money during the coffee course; my daughter asked for money during the liqueur. My wife didn't ask for anything— we have a joint checking account.

"Shall we go for a drive?" I asked her. I knew she wouldn't go—it was time for her soap opera.

"I don't see what you get out of going for a drive every night, but the car cost a fortune, it has to be used. I'm just less and less attracted to material things," she replied.

The children's cars were blocking the garage door. I moved both cars and parked them in the street, moved my car from the garage and parked it in the street, put the other two cars back in the garage, and closed the door. All this maneuvering left me slightly irritated, but when I saw my car's broad bumpers, their special chrome-plated double reinforcement, I felt my heart race with euphoria. I turned the key in the ignition. It was a powerful motor that generated its strength silently beneath its aerodynamic hood. As always, I left without knowing where I would go. It had to be a deserted street, in this city with more people than flies. Not the Avenida Brasil—too busy. I came to a poorly lighted street, heavy with dark trees, the perfect spot. A man or a woman? It made little difference, really, but no one with the right characteristics appeared. I began to get tense. It always happened that way, and I even liked it—the sense of relief was greater. Then I saw the woman. It could be her, even though women were less exciting because they were easier. She was walking quickly, carrying a package wrapped in cheap paper—something from a bakery or the market. She was wearing a skirt and blouse.

There were trees every twenty yards along the sidewalk, an interesting problem that demanded a great deal of expertise. I turned off the headlights and accelerated. She only realized I was going for her when she heard the sound of the tires hitting the curb. I caught her above the knees, right in the middle of her legs, a bit more toward the left leg—a perfect hit. I heard the impact break the large bones, veered rapidly to the left, shot narrowly past one of the trees, and, tires squealing, skidded back onto the asphalt. The car would go from zero to sixty in less than seven seconds. I could see that the woman's broken body had come to rest covered with blood, on top of the low wall in front of a house.

Back in the garage, I took a good look at the car. I ran my hand lightly over the unmarked fender and bumper with pride. Few people in the world could match my skill driving such a car.

The family was watching television. "Do you feel better after your spin?" my wife asked, lying on the sofa, staring fixedly at the TV screen.

"I'm going to bed," I answered. "Good night everybody. Tomorrow's going to be a rough day at the office."

Translated by Clifford E. Landers

Truthful Lies

Frankie McMillan

'M A TRUTHFUL liar, believe you me. You could cut out my heart and throw it to the dogs but I still couldn't give you the bare facts.

Ask me what I had for breakfast. Go on. I'll say what you want to hear: something ordinary and safe. Like Weetabix with chopped banana, milk and a teaspoon of brown sugar. Toast, whole grain with Marmite. You'll understand that. You'll think I'm just the same as you. Okay, now ask me something personal. Go on.

Have I ever been engaged to a dwarf? Yes. No. Choose yes.

His name was Stan and he wore a black suit and had to jump for the door handles. He jumped with both feet so you could see the pink flesh between sock and suit leg. The door would swing open and he'd march on through. The only sign of this little accomplishment was in his hands. For a moment his pudgy hands would flare out like startled starfish. He could kiss. I think his tongue was thicker than normal. Ask me. Ask me what you want to know.

He had special shoes made; his feet weren't long but his fat toes made them wide. Stan could have worn sandals. Get a pair of Roman sandals I told him. No one wears brogues anymore. Only dentists who commit suicide wear brogues.

Ask me about my kids. One day I'll tell you I had four kids. Another day I'll say three. So what happened to the fourth one? Look at me. Watch my cheeks, not my eyes. See the two bright spots of color? That's blood coming to the surface. I'll tell you I lost him. You'll think I was careless. Left baby on the bus. Or at kindy with a stranger in a checked shirt, open necked.

My baby was born in a garage. Stan and me did it up— had Frank Zappa posters on the wall, a batik cloth hung over the ceiling.

Looking at the colors while I was pushing the baby out. Stan running for the doctor because there wasn't a phone and next door didn't want a fuckin' circus on their hands. The dog licking the baby clean and me laughing and crying and not knowing if dogs should be licking newborn babies.

You asked. You wanted to know. Anyway he died. The dog—run over by the milk truck. He was a good dog. Stan took the baby because it was the same as him. Ran off with the baby one night. It was raining. He had an umbrella. You wouldn't think a man would run off carrying an umbrella and a week-old baby boy. Stan did.

My breasts leaked milk for months. The mattress smelt of stale milk; the smell followed me everywhere.

People understand lies. I lost my baby. I had a miscarriage. A loving lie gives you a picture in the head. A dwarf, an umbrella, a garage will give you a headache. You will look at me sideways. You will wonder if I've lost the plot.

I lied when I told you I was lying. You knew that. I let you think that I was lying in order to lie some more but you knew. Because you lie too. Your lies are trivial lies.

Tell me you're made of truthful lies. Let me believe in the goodness of your lying. Go on. Lie. Make it good.

AFGHANISTAN

The Tiger

Mohibullah Zegham

I T WAS MARKET day. I had loaded a dozen sacks of potatoes onto a truck and we were taking them to Kunduz. It had been a long time since I'd been to the bazaar. Traveling the vast Shorao desert, the truck was raising clouds of dust. The desert was so flat that it was hard to believe we were on top of a mountain, and I saw no other vehicles for an hour.

As we descended to Kunduz some armed men in long brown velvet shirts signaled us to stop at a checkpoint. One of them, with his long hair tied back with a handkerchief, came forward. He hovered around the truck for a while, then stopped and wiped his sweaty forehead with a dirty sleeve.

"Who owns these goods?" he demanded, squinting through dusty eyelashes.

"Me," I said.

"Come," he said.

I got down and followed him to an old stronghold where a stream flowed through a courtyard. Silk rugs were spread out beneath large poplar trees. Five men sitting on velvet mattresses were playing dice on a checkered cloth.

Ten or fifteen brown-shirted gunmen sat apart from the game. One of them was puffing hard on a hashish cigarette. "Pull harder, harder!" his companions encouraged him. He puffed again, coughed six or seven times, waved his hands to thank them, then handed it over.

The long-haired gunman was kneeling on the rug now, watching the game.

"You have a lucky hand," he said when one of the players reached in to collect his winnings on the cloth. The other gunmen on the bank of the stream turned their heads and repeated his words.

"Hand it out among the boys," the winner said and threw two bundles of 10,000-Afghani notes toward the long-haired gunman. Then, when he saw me, he said, "Qaleech! Who is that?"

"Sir, he is the owner of the goods."

"What are you carrying?"

"Some potatoes," I replied.

"Where to?"

"To the bazaar, for sale."

"Then you have to pay the tax."

"What tax? I grew these in my own field."

"Qaleech, this man seems a stranger. Do you think he is a spy?"

"By God, I haven't seen him before," Qaleech said, fixing his gaze on me.

I was wondering where I had seen the commander before. His long hair, the beautiful white face, the red lips, the eyes skillfully darkened with kohl, and the soft feminine voice— all were quite familiar to me.

Then I remembered. This was Feroz. His thin moustache, the few hairs of beard on his chin, the long shirt, and the ammunition belt around his waist had changed him entirely.

Feroz had been Haji Murad Bai's keeper and dancing boy.

It had been a long time since I'd seen him. Years ago, Haji Murad would invite us to his house, where Feroz would appear wearing ankle-bells, a woman's costume, powder on his cheeks, lipstick on his lips, henna on his hands, eyes darkened with kohl, and he would dance for us.

Five years ago, rumors spread that Feroz had shot Murad Bai dead and eloped with his younger wife with whom he was having an affair. Murad had won his younger wife, the same age as his daughter, in a partridge-fighting competition. I had heard rumors that Feroz then became a commander of a militant organization, but I didn't know any details.

"I am asking who you are and for whom you are spying?" Feroz's voice brought me out of my thoughts.

"I am Qadoos," I said, "a friend of Murad Bai. Feroz, don't you recognize . . ." A hard blow hit my shoulder before I could finish. Suddenly I was flat on the ground, and then I was being beaten and kicked and hit with rifle butts.

After a few minutes the long-haired gunman pulled me up by my hair to face Feroz but I couldn't. The pain was too fierce. Feroz looked at me furiously and chewed his words to make his voice hoarse.

"Who am I?" he asked.

"You are Feroz," I said.

He hit my mouth with all his force. "No! I am a commander," he shouted. "I am the Tiger!"

Translated by Rashid Khattak

Everyone Out of the Pool

Robert Lopez

THE CLOSEST THING to tumbleweed in New York City is the people.

I say this out loud to the woman next to me because I think she is from Arizona.

Whenever it starts to rain I think end of the world. Whenever the telephone rings or someone calls me by name I think Leonidas at Thermopylae or Custer at Little Bighorn.

What this speaks to I try not to think about.

Don't try to trick me into being happy, is what the woman says back.

We are in a museum when we say this to each other. This particular room in the museum has windows for walls and you can see the weather from anywhere inside it.

This is not just me talking, I say. I pause a moment and then keep talking about the weather until I hear myself say, One bolt of lightning and it's everyone out of the pool time.

I think I've known this woman for years. I think we met in college and have tried since then to get away from each other. The problem is one or the other of us has nothing better to do at any given time. Then I think we came to New York two months ago to help the poor or feed the poor, something with the poor.

The trouble with me is I think too much and don't know anything.

I don't know why this is, though I suspect it's my own fault.

Outside the rain is coming down like it's angry with someone. Like someone had made fun of the rain's mother.

We are sitting on a bench surrounded by twenty giant speakers arranged in an oval. From the speakers a children's choir sings in a foreign language that might be Latin. When you walk from speaker to speaker you hear a different voice, which is why it's in the museum, I think. When you are outside the oval you can't distinguish one voice from the next. To me, the voices all sound the same, even the different ones.

The woman next to me is looking out the window, watching the passersby tramp through gaping puddles, watching the rain like she's never seen it fall down before.

This is when I say something about the homeless, something that sounds like at least they'll have a bath today. Why I say this is because I don't know how she'll react and I'm curious.

Between the choirboys and rainfall the woman can't hear me, though, and from the look on her face I can tell she's making her mind up about something, something that might include leaving me here on this bench to go play in the rain, eventually finding her way west to feed the poor of Tempe or Phoenix or wherever it is she's from and that maybe if I'm lucky she'll call when she gets there.

The Baby

María Negroni

M Y BABY IS playing in the bath, delighted. I begin to wash his head and spend some time at this. Then he begins. When I start to rinse his hair, I can't find him. I turn around, and there he is again. I don't understand what is happening, and grow stern. I scold him. I don't like what he's doing. The baby laughs, more and more amused, glimmers for an instant and vanishes again. My impatience only makes things worse. He disappears more and more quickly, doesn't even give me time to protest. Through layers of uneasiness, I glimpse his mischievous glance; my blindness is his victory, my jealousy his passion. For a while, I go on resisting: I don't know how to welcome impotence. The baby just wants to play. The game is dazzling and lasts a lifetime.

Translated by Anne Twitty

Aglaglagl

Bruce Holland Rogers

Lᴜᴛᴛʟᴇ Gáʙᴏʀ ʟᴏᴏᴋꜱ like any other baby, a fat Bud-dha whose eyes roll this way and that because he hasn't learned the trick of aiming his gaze. He can't even lift the weight of his own head to look around, so his parents aren't to blame for thinking of him as a blank sheet of paper on which they will write, lovingly, all that they know about the world.

But ever since he opened his eyes to the bright air, ever since his fingers first closed accidentally around his mother's finger, a bit of blanket, or the edge of his basinette, Gábor has been thinking. The dog's nose is here, then it is not, then it is here again. Voices come and go. Faces are the same and different. Light alternates with darkness. Wet alternates with dry. He wants milk. He doesn't want milk. A crying sound comes from somewhere, and startles him, and then more crying comes. He has been making inferences, figuring out what it is to Be. He invents a language that contains all of his awareness. His sentences are marvelously efficient, each one containing a whole chapter of his philosophy. *Aglaglagl* is one. He says it when the dog's nose comes to visit the basinette.

Aglaglagl strikes Gábor's parents as a sound of contentment, but they don't know just how right they are. *Aglaglagl* contains what any number of wise men have tried to write in their holy texts using languages entirely unsuited to say *Aglaglagl*.

When Gábor's father leans his face close enough for Gábor to grasp his nose and says *Aglaglagl*, even though he mispronounces it, a squeal of happiness happens. Yes! Aglaglagl! The nature of being, not being, and the dance between them!

It will be some time before Gábor will find that he must learn a second language, a language so broken and unrealistic that in mastering its false categories he will, word by word, learn that he is Gábor, learn that the dog's nose is not a part of him, learn that flowing water is *river* or *Duna* or *Danube*. In acquiring the razors of such language, he will forget nearly everything that he once knew.

The Five New Sons

Zakaria Tamer

THE MARRIAGE OF Abdel Sattar and Laila was a clamorous event in which everyone in the neighborhood took part, but he was not destined to complete his honeymoon. Three days into it he was put under temporary arrest, and when he was released ten years later everyone in the neighborhood—men, women, and children—were there waiting for him. No sooner did they catch a glimpse of him coming through the gate than the women broke into trills of joy, the boys raised a din, and the men rushed to embrace him warmly and congratulate him with words coming straight from the heart. He thanked them all in a trembling voice that could barely be heard for the clamor. But all this din ceased when he scanned the crowd for his wife and saw her standing there, surrounded by five children of different ages, shapes and sizes—fat, thin, short, tall, with fair and dark complexions, and with blond and black hair. Laila saw him looking at her and waved with one hand while the other wiped away the tears. He approached her, his heart beating wildly, and with both hands reached out to the small, soft hand that was wiping away the tears and took it as if it were held out to rescue someone about to drown.

Abdel Sattar stared at Laila in amazement, for she had grown more beautiful and youthful, and looked much younger than her age. The neighborhood folk shouted back and forth in make-believe disapproval, but Abdel Sattar laughed and said, "Legally she's my wife. Have you forgotten that I married her according to the laws of God and His Prophet?"

The noise got louder as it mingled with laughter, and they walked with him to his house. Once there he sat in the shade of the bitter orange tree in the courtyard and sipped his coffee slowly. Suddenly he pointed with his index finger to the five children who were standing apart from him, some eyeing him with hostility and others with shy looks, and said, "Who are these children? Are they the children of neighbors, or relatives?"

His wife immediately started praising the neighborhood for its manliness and gallantry because it had fulfilled its obligation and provided well for a woman who had lost her family and was living alone. Abdel Sattar interrupted, asking her about the children again. She gave him a look of amazement and surprise. "What a question!" she said. "Poor man! Don't you recognize your children? It's true that prison weakens the memory." Abdel Sattar said in a questioning voice, "Were you pregnant when I was arrested?"

"No," Laila answered. "I wasn't pregnant. What a shame! As you remember, the honeymoon lasted only three days, and we were bashful."

Then Laila sighed and said, "But there's no other place like our neighborhood. Do you know Mr. Said, the elementary school teacher? He was the one who volunteered to help me with the first child. Men like him are rare. I can't describe to you the trouble he went to."

"And the second son?" Abdel Sattar asked.

"Look at him closely," Laila answered, "and you can tell right away who helped me with him. There's only one man in our neighborhood with blond hair, Abdel Hafez, the notable. He helped me even though he is married to two insatiable women."

"And the third?" asked Abdel Sattar.

"You know the man who helped me with this one," Laila answered, "and you will approve of my choice: morality, piety, fasting, pilgrimage, and prayer every time the call to prayer is made. Perhaps our son will inherit some of these virtues."

"And the fourth?" asked Abdel Sattar.

"I'm fairly sure the help came from the doctor," Laila answered. "I remember he used to make sure that all drugs for me and the children were free."

"And the fifth?" asked Abdel Sattar.

"You and I don't like a liar," Laila answered. "I'm at a loss to know who was the father in this case due to all the help I got from ten young men or more, each of them taller than a palm tree and wider than a door." Abdel Sattar's fingers let go of the coffee cup, which fell to the ground and shattered, and he squatted against a wall made of rough black stone. He wanted to cry, as he had cried when beaten severely in prison, but his eyes remained dry.

Translated by Ibrahim Muhawi

Appears as #22 in *Breaking Knees*

The Vending Machine at the End of the World

Josephine Rowe

H E MOVED INTO a hotel with my name and called most nights from the pay phone in the hallway. Before that he used to call from a phone box on the corner of Second Avenue and Pine, and I could always hear sirens in the background, and drunks shouting at each other. *Fuck you motherfuckers, I can fly.* That was when he was sleeping in a park at night, and working during the day selling tickets over the phone for the Seattle Opera. The money he earned selling opera tickets he spent on beer and international phone cards. Then he cut down on beer and moved into the hotel that had my name. That kind of love scared the hell out of me. The kind of love that makes a person cut down on beer and move into a hotel just because of its name.

When he called it was nearly midnight for me but early morning for him. I lay on my stomach on the ugly gray carpet of the house that I grew up in, the phone cord stretched to the front door so I could blow cigarette smoke through the wire screen. I imagined him sitting with his face to the wall, ignoring the other residents as they tramped along the hallway. I imagined he still looked a little homeless. JFK once stayed here, he told me, Elvis stayed here. But now the cage elevators were breaking down twice, three times a week and it was fourteen flights of stairs to the room that housed his unrefrigerated forties and his stolen desk.

His two favorite topics of conversation were the Lesser Prairie Chicken, and a vending machine in Fremont that stood alone in the middle of a vacant block. The vending machine had an unlabeled mystery button underneath all of the labeled buttons for the usual drinks. He liked to speculate about what kind of soda would be dispensed if he were to push the mystery button. Would it be Tab or would it be Mr. Pibb? He rattled off a list of dead cola brands from his childhood, most of which I didn't recognize because his childhood was eleven years earlier than mine, and on the other side of the world.

I bet it's Tab, he finally said. He had turned the vending machine into a time-traveling device. He wanted a Tab summer. He wanted it to be 1982 in Atlanta, Georgia, before the methadone trips to Mexico and the minor prison stints for DUI. He wanted to be on his uncle's farm, raising Lesser Prairie Chickens. He wanted to be anywhere but Seattle, selling tickets for the opera.

One night he called and told me he'd gone to Fremont. He'd pushed the mystery button on the vending machine at the end of the world.

And you know what I got?

What'd you get? I asked.

Fucking Sprite.

And Atlanta, Georgia, in 1982 was bleached-out and unreachable and he and I had one less thing to talk about.

The Past

Juan Carlos Botero

HE AWOKE: THE faint sound of tears had finally penetrated the shell of his sleep. He opened his eyes, puzzled. Through the bare window he took in the pale bright night and thought to himself that day would soon break. Only then did he realize she was crying. He rolled over in bed to look at her. "What's the matter?" he asked. His tongue felt furry and numbed by sleep. In the half-light he could make out her naked back, trembling, the sheet crumpled around her waist. He squeezed her shoulder. "What the hell's the matter?" She attempted to calm herself. She sat up in bed cross-legged and dried her tears with the corner of the sheet. She looked at him for a long time then finally unburdened herself of the weight of her suffering. "For a year now I've been seeing someone else," she pronounced in a broken voice. "We're going to get married." And then she broke down, crying uncontrollably, tearing at her hair and wailing: "It's horrible. *Horrible!*" He went cold. He stared at her in astonishment, not managing to pinpoint his feelings. Suddenly, the past year seemed to turn in his memory. The

whole series of events rotated as in a kaleidoscope until settling on an inconceivable and yet irrefutable image. So: all
the times she visited her mother, the weekends when work
kept her away from him, the times she got back late from
the office, the times the phone rang and she hung up after
saying "wrong number," began stripping themselves of their
innocence and assumed new meanings, ones with cast-iron
signs of betrayal. Now, he discovered, his memory was stor-
ing *another* past. He experienced a painful prick to the heart
but, before it shattered to pieces, he began to see that the
past was not a fixed route, rigid and frozen in time, as he
had always believed, but rather quite the opposite, a fragile
journey, malleable and, above all, *vulnerable*. Just one phrase,
he realized, could alter the whole past.

Translated by Jethro Soutar
and Anne McLean

Everyone Does Integral Calculus

Kuzhali Manickavel

AFTER WE LOOKED at the sea, Durai and I turned and looked at the highway. He said the sea would blind us if we stared at it too long. The highway would just make us sad or put us to sleep. We looked at the roadkill and decided to take stock of ourselves. "Let's retrace the journey, right from the beginning," said Durai. "What did we do to get here?"

Durai went first. He said that when he was a boy he sang devotional songs and his eyes would close of their own accord when he sang the word "God."

"Sing something now," I said. "Anything."

"No."

"Oh come on. It doesn't have to be about God. Something small. One line."

He rubbed his face and looked over his shoulder at the sea. Then he sang softly in Tamil. *"You're just a doll, I'm just a doll, when you think about it, we're all just dolls."*

I noticed strings of nits shining like beads in his hair.

"Well?" he said.

"You couldn't think of anything else to sing?" I said.

I wanted to know why Durai didn't sing anymore.

"Something must have happened," I said. "Someone must have abused you musically."

"Okay, your turn. What did you do to get here?"

"Nothing."

"Think. You must have done something."

"Integral calculus."

"That doesn't count. Everyone does integral calculus."

"Not everyone. Not poor people."

"Even poor people. If they go to school, they do integral calculus."

I thought of picking a louse from his hair when he wasn't looking. I thought of how it would squirm in the center of my palm like a tiny misshapen star.

Durai said we were not getting anywhere so he suggested secrets.

"Okay go," I said.

"I got thrown in jail when I was in college."

"So?"

"What so? It was jail. Like jail-jail, with bars and shit."

"All guys get thrown in jail when they're in college. They also become drug addicts and fall in love with prostitutes."

"You forgot the motorcycles. We all had motorcycles."

"When I was little I really wanted to be a boy. I wanted to have a name like Sathya and wear hats and sunglasses."

Durai scratched the inside of his wrist in slow, straight lines, like he was trying to open a vein.

"Do you still wish you were a boy?" he asked.

"No. Once my breasts kicked in I changed my mind."

"That's good. I like your breasts."
"I know you do."

We were still facing the road but our heads had turned and we were looking at the sea again. We discovered that we had both stolen mercury from our school chemistry labs. Durai had slipped his into his pocket. I had hidden mine in my geometry box. We both had rolled it across our hands and face. I was sure we would get cancer because of this but Durai said it would just make us go crazy. I leaned back and thought about the lice sucking and fucking on his head.

"My neck hurts. Why can't we just face the sea?" I said.

"It's too soon."

"What's that song? About coming too soon or too early? Tickticktick something something?"

"No idea," said Durai.

"Are you sure? I thought everyone knew that song."

I yawned and watched a thick, black louse clamber up through his hair and wave desperately at the sky.

Little Girls

Tara Laskowski

Jane's dad calls while she is out hanging clothes, his voice staccato over the cell. He had heard a story about a woman, a professional violinist. She slipped and fell on the open dishwasher. She sliced her arm open on a knife. She would probably never play again.

Jane props the skinny phone between her ear and shoulder and lets her dad's words flutter, the clothespins pinching her fingertips. One of the pins falls from her mouth and tumbles down the incline to her neighbor's fence, where it will stay until someone else rescues it. It is sticky for early June, and the grass feels like straw on her bare toes.

"I want you to be careful, Janie," her father says, and she pictures him in his car, windows down, speeding with a cigarette in his mouth. He tells her that life is full of danger, everywhere, anywhere. "Watch out for knives and power tools."

She laughs, imagining her body vibrating above a jack-hammer, her arms wielding a heavy chain saw through the wall of the nursery-in-progress upstairs, the nursery her husband is painting light green. A wave of nausea, common now these past few days, makes her nearly drop the phone. "I have to go," she tells her father. She takes a break and kneels down, pressing fingers on her belly.

A girl, she thinks. Perhaps she will be famous—a doctor, a writer. A musician, like the violinist. But the violinist thought she was safe in her kitchen—one second booking concerts over a tasty chicken dinner, then a cat, a skid, then blood, lots of it—hadn't her parents ever told her never to load the knives blade-up? Someone had to have told her that sometime. People were always eager to dispense advice like gumballs—push, pop, chew.

Her husband calls to her from their back porch. She shades her eyes from the sun, and he mistakes it for a wave. She sees the hill before her as if for the first time now, so steep, a quandary they had pondered when they bought the place many years ago, when her husband had promised he would build a swimming pool into the side of it, put some steps in to make it easier to navigate. She takes a step toward him, her legs a pair of trembling horsehair strings. She can feel her fall as if it has already happened—the blades of grass pressing into her side, not bending to her weight but stabbing. And her husband just far enough away, his hand still bent in a wave, smiling, likely thinking of pale green and quiet lullabies.

Ronggeng

Yin Ee Kiong

Dark clouds and high winds; unmistakable signs of the impending monsoon. Soon sky and earth will marry and bring forth bountiful harvests. But before that there must be ronggeng.

Ronggeng is in the soul of every Sundanese; they dance it beautifully. But only one would carry the indang of Ki Secamenggala, the spirit of ronggeng.

Ki Secamenggala had whispered into the little heart of Ratih, breathed his breath into her soul.

To be chosen "Ronggeng Princess" meant more than just honor for her family. All the rich old men in their vulgar boast of wealth and virility would be vying to buka her kelambu—"to open her mosquito net"—for the first time at the ronggeng.

Like the meeting of sky and earth it would bring bountiful wealth to Ratih's family.

After her ritual bath in the river Ratih was piggybacked home so her feet would not touch the ground till the ronggeng. Kalsom, still a beauty and a ronggeng princess in her day, prepared Ratih for the evening. She painted her granddaughter's lips vermillion with sirih and applied a concoction of turmeric and coconut oil on Ratih's face and arms so that they glistened golden. She wrapped her small body with the incipient breasts of a thirteen-year-old in the finest songket, gold threaded to shimmer with every move of Ratih's body. The child's hair was done in a chignon held in place with a golden pin.

Djoko thought his heart would burst with the pounding as he witnessed all this from the crack in the floor from under the house. He had loved Ratih from the day she danced the ronggeng as a little girl, while he and his friends mimicked the various instruments with their mouths. Why should the rich get everything?

The music started; the other girls danced. Young men who could not afford the bidding took to the floor to try their chances.

It would soon be Ratih's turn. Kalsom hurried out of the room to pick the nocturnal-blooming ylangylang for Ratih's hair.

Djoko saw his chance. He climbed in through the window.

Meanwhile the beat quickened with the dancers climaxing to a crescendo of gong and cymbals.

"Ayo!" Kalsom shrieked when she saw the two as one on the floor. "We are ruined."

They would surely be ruined if it became known that Ratih's mosquito net had been rendered. She had a mind to kill Djoko but there were more urgent things to do.

Kalsom repaired Ratih's makeup, wrapped her in the songket again and tended to her hair, this time with the flower crowning her chignon. She breathed a spell on Ratih's crown as she sent her out.

A hush came over the crowd as Ratih emerged. Her

movements flowed with the music. Delicate fingers waved their magic as her hips swayed back and forth to the suggestive syncopation. Her eyes seduced the bidders, speaking to each alone as she recited lewd lyrics in Ki Secamenggala's voice. The oil lamps flickered, dancing with Ratih, casting shadows sinuously.

She danced to the pulsating rhythm in a ronggeng so exquisite none could remember better. The old men nodded their agreement that she surpassed even Kalsom.

Razak started the bidding with an extravagant flourish of two gold coins. Baginda countered with two gold coins and a buffalo. Khalid upped by another buffalo. Intoxicated by the drinks and the heady fragrance of the ylangylang, Razak decided to end the charade. He threw in another two gold coins and expansively added five buffaloes, to gasps from the crowd and the good-natured backslapping of the other bidders, who gave up.

While Ratih mesmerized the crowd Kalsom prepared herself. She was almost her granddaughter's size and discounting the ravages of time was in every way Ratih. Kalsom blew out all the oil lamps except one. She bundled Ratih out of the house as soon as she had finished, to the waiting Djoko.

Bumbling past the curtains with swagger to spare Razak looked uncertainly at the figure before him. Kalsom looked him in the eye and muttered the mantra the shaman taught her when he implanted the susuk—a sliver of gold—in the middle of her forehead. Blinded by the beauty before him Razak reached for her but she demurred. The blushing Kalsom eventually relented allowing Razak to buka her kelambu.

Razak was aghast when he woke up next to Kalsom. She smiled. He grimaced.

But who was he going to tell?

Butterfly Forever

Chen Qiyou

T IS RAINING. The asphalt road looks cold and wet. It glitters with reflections of green, yellow, and red lights. We are taking shelter under the balcony. The green mailbox stands alone across the street. Inside the big pocket of my white windbreaker is a letter for my mother in the South.

Yingzi says she can mail the letter for me with the umbrella. I nod quietly and hand her the letter.

"Who told us to bring only one small umbrella?" She smiles, opens up the umbrellla, and is ready to walk across the road to mail the letter for me. A few tiny raindrops from an umbrella rib fall onto my glasses.

With the piercing sound of a vehicle screeching to a halt, Yingzi's life flies in the air gently, and then slowly falls back on the cold and wet road, like a butterfly at night.

Although it is spring, it feels like deep autumn.

All she did was cross the road to mail a letter for me. A very simple act, yet I will never forget it as long as I live.

I open my eyes and remain standing under the balcony, blankly, my eyes filled with hot tears. All the cars in the entire world have stopped. People rush to the middle of the road. Nobody knows the one that lies on the road there is mine, my butterfly. At this moment she is only five meters away from me, yet it is so far away. Bigger raindrops fall onto my glasses, splashing into my life.

Why? Why did we bring only one umbrella?

Then I see Yingzi again, in her white windbreaker, the umbrella above her head, crossing the road quietly. She is mailing the letter for me. The letter I wrote to my mother in the South. I stand blankly under the balcony and see, once again, Yingzi walking toward the middle of the road.

The rain wasn't that big, yet it was the biggest rain in my entire life. Below is the content of the letter. Did Yingzi know?

"Ma, I am going to marry Yingzi next month."

Translated by Shouhua Qi

Labyrinth

Juan José Barrientos

L ABYRINTHS ARE DESIGNED to make it difficult or impossible for those who venture into them to find the exit. But a very different building exists.

Those who have entered it remember the usual corridors, turns, and staircases, but also the murmur of a party, of muted laughter, furtive comments, the tinkling of glasses or silverware, sometimes the panting of secret lovers, the burst of an orchestra or jazz combo or at least a melody interpreted by a solitary piano.

Upon hearing them, they hurry to draw near, but the strange architecture, not devoid of traps and pitfalls, sends them down a chute like trespassers onto the street.

From there they look back at the bright and inaccessible celebration, where it seems that everything is happiness.

Translated by Juan José Barrientos
and Gwen Shapard

The Light Eater

Kirsty Logan

I T BEGAN WITH the Christmas tree lights. They were candy-bright, mouth-size. She wanted to feel the lightness of them on her tongue, the spark on her taste buds. Without him life was so dark, and all the holiday debris only made it worse. She promised herself she wouldn't bite down.

The bulb was sweet and sharp, and it slid down her throat with a feeling of relief: an itch finally scratched. She came to with a shock. At the realization of what she'd done, she tangled the lights back into their box and pushed them onto the highest shelf. The next day she pulled down the box and ate the rest. The power cable was slippery as licorice.

She got hungrier as the days passed. A lightbulb blew; she went to change it but ended up sucking it like a gobstopper. She had soon eaten the rest of the bulbs in the house. Lamps mushroomed up from every flat surface—and there's no good in a darkened light. Each day she visited the hardware shop and walked home with bags full to clinking. Her eyes were always full of light; with each blink she caught gold on her eyelashes.

One night she opened her mouth to yawn, and saw that her path was lit. Up she jumped, pajamaed and barefoot, and followed the light across streets and playgrounds, fields and forests, all the way to the edge of the land.

She paused on the rocks, between the trees at her back and the black of the sea. This is where he left, and this is where she could find him again. She stretched her body to the sky in readiness, then opened her mouth to outshine the stars.

She spat out the bulbs—one, two; nineteen, twenty—in a runway from trees to shore. She spread herself out on the sand. A perfect starfish, a fallen body. An X, so he could find his way back.

Late for Dinner

Jim Crace

THERE IS NO greater pleasure than to be expected at a meal and not arrive.

While the first guests were standing in the villa's lobby with their wet hair and their dry wine, their early efforts at a conversation saved and threatened by fresh arrivals at the door, he was driving slowly in the rain along the coastal highway, enjoying his loud absence from the room, enjoying— first, the cranes and depots of the port, and then the latest condominiums, the half-glimpsed bypassed villages with their dead roads, the banks of coastal gravel, the wind, the darkness, and the trees.

While they were being seated at the dining table and were thinking—those who knew him—Lui's always late, he was taking pleasure from the water on the tarmac, the old movie romance of the windscreen wipers and the dashboard lights, the prospect of the speedy, starless, hungry night ahead.

At what point would his sister or her husband, George, dial his home, discreetly from another room, only to get the answer phone and leave the message . . . What? Was he okay? Had he forgotten that they'd asked him round to eat with friends? Would he come late? Was he aware what trouble he'd put them to? Would he arrive in time to charm the sweet young teacher that they'd found and placed at his left elbow?

At what point would his plate, his napkin, and his cutlery be gathered up and two women asked to shift their chairs along to fill his place and break the gendered pattern of the table?

At what point would his hostess say, It's not like him at all?

While they were eating in his absence—a sweet corn soup, a choice of paddock lamb or vegetarian risotto, Mother Flimsy's tart with brandy—he was driving with one hand and, with the other, breaking pieces off his chocolate bar. He was dreaming repartee and dreaming manners-of-a-king and being far the smartest, sharpest person in the room.

While they were sitting in his sister's long salon, for coffee and a little nip of Boulevard liqueur, and getting cross about some small remark their host had made at their expense, Lui reached the hundred-kilometer mark that he had set himself. He took the exit from the highway, slowed down to drive the narrow underpass—sixty sobering meters of bright lights, dry road, wind-corralled litter, a couple sheltering—and turned onto the opposite lane. He headed back toward the town and home, another hundred k, a hundred k less cinematic, less romantic, and more futile than the journey out.

The rain, now coming from the right, presented unexpected angles for the car. It tilted at the windscreen with more percussion than before. He had to put his wipers on their fastest setting. The smell was weather, chocolate, gasoline. The skyline warmed and lifted with its fast-advancing lights, those attic rooms, those bars, those streets, those television sets, those sweeping cars and cabs, those marriages that brighten up the night.

His eyes were sore and tired. His mouth was dry. He'd have to concentrate to take his pleasure from the drive, his safe and happy absence from the room, his prudent, timid, well-earned thirst. He put a steady glass up to his lips and sipped. Dipped his spoon into the sweet corn soup. Chose the lamb. Nodded at the windscreen wipers for a second helping of the tart. How witty he could be, how certain in his views, how helpful with the wine, how neat and promising. The pretty woman on his left extended her slim arm and squeezed his hand by way of thanks for his good company, and slipped out of the room into his car, a passenger, an absentee, the gender pattern at the table restored. He broke his chocolate bar in half and shared with her the unfed midnight journey into town.

Appears as #36 in *The Devil's Larder*

Volcanic Fireflies

Mónica Lavín

ADAPTED TO POPOCATÉPETL'S sulfurous crater, this species of Coleoptera is endemic to the Valley of Mexico. It wasn't reported in the literature until 1994, when Metro maintenance personnel encountered hundreds of fragile and sickly insects deposited between the tracks. Urban entomologists, long buried in routine fly and tick epidemics, were astonished by the golden powder emanating from the creatures, along with their signature stench, more typical of mineral springs than insects. With rigorous fieldwork—if that's what you call nocturnal strolls in Metro stations—the scientists officially experienced the nighttime flickering glow of what we now know as the volcanic firefly.

Sophisticated chemical reactions catalyzed by sulfur are responsible for the luminescence of these inhabitants of the volcano's crater, with its darkness, high temperatures and boiling lava. Old as the volcano itself, the creatures have now, for whatever reason, spread to the luminous space of the valley. Perhaps forced out by new gaseous vapors or volatile cinders, perhaps fugitive for generations, some subset

found, in the blackness of Metro tunnels, the temperatures
that enable them—after metabolizing the sulfur oxide of the
contaminated atmosphere—to glow brightly and reproduce
in an anonymity only recently violated. Magnification first
revealed the eyes of these amber insects as fatigued, aged,
with growths in their surface membrane. Fine electrodes
detected a violent interior vibration, as if the insects' vital
liquids were imitating the gurgling of lava. Since then, people have given generous donations for the preservation of
this species, born of volcanic activity, as it seeks the metrop-
olis. A high-risk aerial expedition is planned—by the more
romantic entomologists, if this branch of study admits such
inclination—to lower some of these insects into the cone
of the crater, protected in an asbestos cage, to observe their
capacity for re-adaptation. But the more skeptical—always
the most realistic—think that it's pointless, given the change
already in progress. Golden and potbellied, volcanic fireflies have taken flight on theater stages, in actors' dressing
rooms, in corners of the red-light district and in bars. With
vestigial auras of a volcanic past that's moved its vertigo to
another setting, they can be found wherever the smell of sulfur abounds and under the microscope now exhibit a young
and lascivious look.

Translated by Patricia Dubrava

CUBA

Insomnia

Virgilio Piñera

THE MAN GOES to bed early but he cannot fall asleep. He turns and tosses. He twists the sheets. He lights a cigarette. He reads a bit. He puts out the light again. But he cannot sleep. At three in the morning he gets up. He calls on his friend next door and confides in him that he cannot sleep. He asks for advice. The friend suggests he take a walk and maybe he will tire himself out—then he should drink a cup of linden tea and turn out the light. He does all these things but he does not manage to fall asleep. Again he gets up. This time he goes to see the doctor. As usual the doctor talks a good deal but in the end the man still cannot manage to sleep. At six in the morning he loads a revolver and blows out his brains. The man is dead but still he is unable to sleep. Insomnia is a very persistent thing.

Translated by Alberto Manguel

Four Hands

Margarita Meklina

MOTHER: A SHORT, black-haired jackdaw, she cordially opens mouth, door, piano. She walks right in, sits, begins playing right off. Bravo, Nonna, says her husband. It really is bravura. On the walls: candelabras and handicrafts created from nature's cornucopia. Gay elation: "Know what I'm playing?" then acute condemnation: "Surely you're joking, not the boyish Shainsky! It's Chopin!"

The parting gift's a shell, an abalone. She's drawn to the cradle the guests brought. "I keep telling mine to try, but they're in no hurry to make a grandma out of me!" An ostensibly joking nod to her weak son—some software specialist—and his strong, muscular wife.

Father: Looks like a bowlegged Cossack. Used to be a first-class pianist too, but ruined his reach (fishing), his back (sciatica), and the joy of music (drinking). Now he fiddles with his boat, named in honor of his black-haired helpmeet. There's pictures of him and his catfish: he's happy and bewhiskered, the catfish has whiskers too, but is dead. Father lives, but without will, like the forte pedal under his wife's foot. He hems and haws in parting; he's spackling, fudging it, fixing his oarlocks as he sits on the hull.

Son: A child soloist, went on stage with the orchestra (coughing in the auditorium, parents stock-still), then abandoned the bow to bond with the Italian people. On the way through Italy to the States he washed cars, hawked pins and mangy matreshka dolls on the sidewalk, and now he's afraid of everything: of being alone, of being single, of his mother's fury, his father's indifference.

Son's Wife: They had the wedding on a boat that all the white trash could fit on. Fraternization of intellectual Soviet Jews with the wife's brother and cousin: arrogant American soldier-boy who went AWOL twice, slutty secretary. The young wife had three pairs of parents, all rednecks: her father—knobby head, shit-kicker boots—got serially divorced.

After the wedding: a rented apartment, shelter dogs (biters, who after a few training sessions at fifty bucks a pop had to be put down), snow and skis in Sierra Nevada, rest and sun in Israel, trips to India, Japan, Katmandu. Finally: their own home, with a stubbornly leaky faucet. Son reports to mother: yes, I bought a house, no, I haven't fixed the pipes yet.

Mother anxiously awaits a grandchild. The first few tries are failures, but finally, the belly appears and swells serenely. In the sixth month the

Wife announced that she's a lesbian.

Mother says that she refuses to have anything to do with a daughter-in-law like this, and

Father, with his catatonic, photogenic catfish, just repeats after the mother and continues floating on the boat named after her.

Son is in total shock. Got to fix the faucet and sell the house. Got to find another wife, and fast (he can't make it alone, but he'd had all kinds of girls in bed before the wedding: students with improbable majors, spiteful ice queens, pimply nothing-muches with their salicylic acid).

<u>Wife</u>: Wanted to get married to be like everybody else, "to have a real wedding too, with guests, with nice stuff," and so tried to smother all feeling for women, but she couldn't do a thing about it.

<u>Son</u> is in shock.

<u>Mother</u> and <u>Father</u> are in total denial: she's not any daughter-in-law of ours, her daughter is no grandchild to us, and if you keep visiting her, you won't be any son to us.

<u>Wife</u>: I wasn't even looking for anything, after all Sonya was already here under my heart, but then I saw Her and knew right away.

<u>Son</u>: My ex-wife and I got together, and I was suddenly struck: how did I get along with her for so long, this completely foreign person? This made me feel a little better, and right then Sonya started knocking . . . just as though she were waiting for me to fly in from Colorado (now we live in different states).

The next morning I got a call and I came right away, and there's my ex-wife in labor, in the bathtub so everything's natural, no anesthesia . . . I was holding her by one hand, and her live-in lover by the other. Then my Sonya came into the world, with her tiny little nose and nails . . . striking how much she looks like me . . .

<u>Mother</u> and <u>Father</u>: We don't have any granddaughter. We don't have any former daughter-in-law. There's no such people.

They go to the piano and play a piece for four hands.

Translated by Anne O. Fisher

Engkanto

Peter Zaragoza Mayshle

ONCE MY STUPID mother brought me to the *arbularyo* who told me to sit in front of him and took out a twig from his pants pocket and placed it against his palm measuring it and he waved it inches from my face and told me to close my eyes and I did and he told me to open my eyes and I did and he placed the twig on his palm and somehow it had grown longer extending a couple of inches past the tip of his middle finger and my mother gasped and he said that indeed an *engkanto* had found favor in me and he told me to lie on the floor and close my eyes and I did and he told my mother to close her eyes too and place her hands on my arms and grip them tightly and she did and I felt his damp hand clamp on my mouth and I felt his tobacco breath on my face and I felt his other hand massaging my breasts and my eyes popped open and I saw him leering down at me and when I tried to shout his hand clamped tighter on my mouth and when I began to squirm and struggle he shouted to my mother to keep her eyes closed and pray harder and hold me tighter for the *engkanto* was trying to break free and I twisted wildly and managed to kick him in the groin and he let out a yelp and I sat up and I looked at my mother and she looked at me both of us breathing heavily and she asked if the *engkanto* was still inside me and he croaked I was cured and my mother promised to send him a pail of crabs from father's next catch and we left him there still holding on to his testicles and I never told my mother about what really happened for when we exchanged looks that day on the *arbularyo*'s floor I only saw benevolence and concern in her eyes unaware of what she had done. I have been her protector ever since.

Without a Net

Ana María Shua

TRAVELING FREAKS

Despised, listless, made into pariahs by the well-intentioned and the defenders of human rights, the freaks who once worked in the circus now wander the world aimlessly. They are the dwarves, bearded women, Siamese twins, pinheads, and snake men, the deformed and crippled individuals of all types who once upon a time would have earned an honorable living in show business. The really notable ones show up on television. Because of the fallout there's a lot of competition.

SURPRISE

We circus performers desperately try to figure out how to surprise the audience. It's not enough to perfect traditional acts. We try, then, to outdo what has gone before: to do a somersault with five turns through the air, juggle with five anvils and five feathers, swallow an umbrella, or a lamppost, to sustain a human pyramid the size of an Egyptian pyramid on the slack wire, to enter a cage with 350 lions and two tigers, to make all the enemies of a randomly chosen audience member disappear.

How to surprise the audience? In the new circuses, they dress up the old tricks with costumes, choreography, lighting, and with acting.

But, as we get older, our bodies can't take the extremes. We're not beautiful enough, funny enough, elastic enough, ingenious enough to get jobs with the new circuses. How to surprise those damn cynical spectators who've seen everything? In an attempt to offer the ultimate show, we let ourselves die on the sand amid the applause, and it's not enough, it's not enough. Anyone can do that.

POLITICAL CORRECTNESS

The pleasure of seeing others risk their lives, the joy of someone else being in danger, is no longer acceptable. Nowadays the trapeze artists use safety wires, the tigers are muzzled, the bears have no claws, the knife thrower hurls his weapons against an outline of a human being.

But in private, when practicing, the circus artists always do things the dangerous way, and the knife thrower boasts of being able to hit his wife or any other woman in the eye from twenty paces.

Translated by Steven J. Stewart

Appointment in Samarra

As retold by W. Somerset Maugham

DEATH SPEAKS:
There was a merchant in Baghdad who sent his servant to market to buy provisions and in a little while the servant came back, white and trembling, and said, Master, just now when I was in the marketplace I was jostled by a woman in the crowd and when I turned I saw it was Death that jostled me. She looked at me and made a threatening gesture; now, lend me your horse, and I will ride away from this city and avoid my fate. I will go to Samarra and there Death will not find me. The merchant lent him his horse, and the servant mounted it, and he dug his spurs in its flanks and as fast as the horse could gallop he went. Then the merchant went down to the marketplace and he saw me standing in the crowd and he came to me and said, Why did you make a threatening gesture to my servant when you saw him this morning? That was not a threatening gesture, I said, it was only a start of surprise. I was astonished to see him in Baghdad, for I had an appointment with him tonight in Samarra.

The Hawk

Brian Doyle

RECENTLY A MAN in my town took up residence on the town football field, in a small tent in the northwestern corner, near the copse of cedars. He had been a terrific football player some years ago for our high school, and then played in college, and then played a couple of years in the nether reaches of the professional ranks, where a man might get paid a hundred bucks a game plus bonuses for touchdowns and sacks, and then he had entered into several business ventures, but these had not gone so well, and he had married and had children, but that had not gone so well either, and finally he took up residence on the football field, because, as he said, that was where things *had* gone well, and while he knew for sure that people thought he was nuts to pitch a tent on the field, he sort of needed to get balanced again, and there was something about the field that was working for him in that way as far as he could tell after a few days, so, with all due respect to people who thought he was a nutcase, he thought he would stay there until someone made him leave. He had already spoken with the cops, he said, and it was a mark of the general decency of our town that he was told he could stay awhile as long as he didn't interfere with use of the field, which of course he would never think of doing such a thing, and it was summer, anyways, so the field wasn't in use much.

He had been nicknamed the Hawk when he was a player, for his habit of lurking around almost lazily on defense and then making a stunning strike, and he still speaks the way he played, quietly but then amazingly, and when we sat on the visiting team's bench the other day he said some quietly amazing things, which I think you should hear.

The reporter from the paper came by the other day, he said, and she wanted to write a story about the failure of the American dream, and the collapse of the social contract, and she was just *melting* to use football as a metaphor for something or other, and I know she was just trying to do her job, but I kept telling her things that didn't fit what she wanted, like that people come by and leave me cookies and sandwiches, and the kids who play lacrosse at night set up a screen so my tent wouldn't get peppered by stray shots, and the cops drift by at night to make sure no one's giving me grief. Everyone gets nailed at some point so we understand someone getting nailed and trying to get back up on his feet again. I am not a drunk and there's no politicians to blame. I just lost my balance. People are good to me. You try to get lined up again. I keep the field clean. Mostly it's discarded water bottles. Lost cell phones I hang in a plastic bag by the gate. I walk the perimeter a lot. I saw coyote pups the other day. I don't have anything smart to say. I don't know what things mean. Things just are what they are. I never sat on the visitors' bench before, did you? Someone leaves coffee for me every morning by the gate. The other day a lady came by with twin infants and she let me hold one while we talked about football. That baby weighed about half of nothing. You couldn't believe a human being could be so tiny, and there were two of him. That reporter, she kept asking me what I had learned, what would I say to her readers if there was one thing to say, and I told her what could possibly be better than standing on a football field holding a brand-new human being the size of a coffee cup, you know what I mean? Everything else is sort of a footnote. If you stay really still at dusk you can see the progression of what's in the sky in order, which is swallows, then swifts, then bats, then owls, then lacrosse balls, and when the lacrosse guys are finished they stop by to say hey and to tell me they are turning off the field lights. Real courteous kids, those kids. If the world to come is going to be run by kids who play lacrosse, I think we are in excellent hands.

The Egg Pyramid

Nuala Ní Chonchúir

THERE ARE THINGS you can do when your husband sleeps with your sister. You can sit in your studio and imagine them together, the toad and the mouse. Him moving over her. Her on top of him. You can hear dark skin slap against honey skin; you can hear moans. But he is *your* toad and she is *your* mouse—your Diego and your Cristina—so you drown those thoughts because they bring more tears than a bloodletting.

But there are things you can do. You can take the pins from your hair and unweave the plaits. Then you can use a scissors to hack off the lengths. You can scatter the strands on the floor and on your yellow chair, where they lie like snakes. The dogs and monkeys—who still love you—can watch. You can forgo silver rings and turquoise beads. You can dress like a man, in a baggy gray suit and maroon shirt. You can hang your Tijuana dresses in the closet and shut the door on their gaiety.

What else can you do? Well, you can imagine his seed nestling in your sister's womb and blossoming. You can witness a baby—a boy, let's say—making a hard melon of her belly. You have never had a ripe stomach. Three times that might have happened for you; three times you bled your baby out before anyone knew that you too could give life. You can look at your sister's children and ask yourself if they have features that belong to your husband—drooping eyes, full lips, cruelty.

You can count up the seven years you have lived together and you can see that there are plenty of itches to be scratched on both sides. You know that Diego's urge to scratch burns more than yours; his need is eternal. You can leave your house and take a flat in the heart of Mexico, to create a space for your husband to sulk into and for your sister to wonder in. You can fly to New York then hurry home again, because Diego pulls on you the way mother moon pulls on the sea.

Your husband is an accident that happened to you but he is also your north and south. And, because you love him more than your own skin, you can try to accept and you can try to forgive. You can shrug off the pain that pinches like a body brace and throw laughter bombs out into the world to blow up the hurt that remains.

But, when your sister sleeps with your husband, it is like balancing a pyramid of eggs on a glass platter on the top of your head. You dare not move much for fear of what might happen. The best thing that you can do is to take your brush in one hand, your palette in the other, and sit at your easel and paint. Yes, you can paint.

An Ouroboric Novel

Giorgio Manganelli

A WOMAN HAS GIVEN birth to a sphere: it's a question of a globe some twenty centimeters in diameter. Delivery was easy, without complications. Whether or not the woman is married is unknown. A husband would have presumed a relationship with the devil, and would have thrown her out of the house, or perhaps would have beaten her to death with a hammer. So, she has no husband. She is said to be a virgin. In any case, she is a good mother: she is very attached to the sphere. Since the sphere has no mouth, she feeds it by immersing it in a small basin filled with her milk. The basin is decorated with flowers. The sphere is perfectly smooth and uninterrupted. It has no eyes, nor any limbs by way of which to move itself, but all the same it rolls about the room, goes up the stairs, bouncing lightly and very gracefully. The material of which it's made is more rigid than flesh, but not completely inelastic. Its movements show will and decision, something that might be referred to as clear ideas. Its mother washes it every day, and feeds it. In reality, it is never dirty. It seems it does not sleep, even though it never disturbs its mother: it emits no sounds. All the same, she believes herself to understand that, in certain moments, the sphere is anxious for her touch; it seems to her that in those moments its surface is softer. People avoid the woman who gave birth to a sphere, but the woman does not notice it. All day long, all night long, her life revolves around the sphere's pathetic perfection. She knows the sphere, no matter how much a prodigy, to be extremely young. She watches it slowly grow. After three months, its diameter has increased by nearly five centimeters. At times its surface, generally gray, takes on a pinkish hue. The mother has nothing to teach the sphere, but tries to learn from it; she follows its movements, attempts to understand if there's something it's "trying to tell her." She has the impression that, no, the sphere has nothing to tell her, but all the same is a part of her. The mother knows the sphere will not remain forever in her home; but this precisely is what touches her: to have been involved in a story both alarming and utterly tranquil. When the days are warm and sunny, she takes the sphere in her arms and goes for a walk outside, around the house. At times she goes as far as a public park, and has the impression that people are getting used to her, to her sphere. She likes to let it roll among the flower beds, to follow it and catch it, with a gesture of fright and passion. The mother loves the sphere, and wonders if ever a woman has been so much a mother as she.

Translated by Henry Martin

That Color

Jon McGregor

S HE STOOD BY the window and said, Those trees are turning that beautiful color again. Is that right, I asked. I was at the back of the house, in the kitchen. I was doing the dishes. The water wasn't hot enough. She said, I don't know what color you'd call it. These were the trees on the other side of the road she was talking about, across the junction. It's a wonder they do so well where they are, with the traffic. I don't know what they are. Some kind of maple or sycamore, perhaps. This happens every year and she always seems taken by surprise. These years get shorter every year. She said, I could look at them all day, I really could. I rested my hands in the water and I listened to her standing there. Her breathing. She didn't say anything. She kept standing there. I emptied the bowl and refilled it with hot water. The room was cold, and the steam poured out of the water and off the dishes. I could feel it on my face. She said, They're not just red, that's not it, is it now. I rinsed off the frying pan and ran my fingers around it to check for grease. My knuckles were starting to ache again, already. She said, When you close your eyes on a sunny day, it's a bit like that color. Her voice was very quiet. I stood still and listened. She said, It's hard to describe. A lorry went past and the whole house shook with it and I heard her step away from the window, the way she does. I asked why she was so surprised. I told her it was autumn, it was what happened: the days get shorter, the chlorophyll breaks down, the leaves turn a different color. I told her she went through this every year. She said, It's just lovely, they're lovely, that's all, you don't have to. I finished the dishes and poured out the water and rinsed the bowl. There was a very red skirt she used to wear, when we were young. She dyed her hair to match it once and some people in the town were moved to comment. Flame-red, she called it then. Perhaps these leaves were like that, the ones she was trying to describe. I dried my hands and went through to the front room and stood beside her. I felt for her hand and held it. I said, But tell me again.

Like a Family

Meg Pokrass

THE CITY IS always moving its pinkie to tell me it's alive. One day it smells like steaming artichokes—another day, lapsang souchong tea. My friends, other secretaries, gather on the sunny bench like a bouquet. From a block away it looks as if they are complaining, bending backwards and yawning. He never liked them, or even wanted to know them, but now that he's not around, they're what I have.

I live on Carl Street near the park in a room big enough for myself and maybe a ferret, a half block from the express train. I work downtown in an office complex where I keep schedules for three generations of architects. For Christmas they gave me a robot dog and a gift certificate to TravelSmith.

My stomach twists like an earthworm after the rain. I tell myself I won't wait for the phone to ring anymore, but have waited all Saturday morning again. When it rings, I count to three, touch "talk."

"Yo Yo Ma," I say.

Calling me is probably on his "to do" list, which I imagine includes trying on new running shoes in preparation for his next marathon, meeting his training coach in her live/ work space, upgrading his phone or his GPS running gizmo, catching up with his ex-wife over Dragonwell tea. Taking the kids for the weekend, so she can play.

"What's new?" he asks.

He's lighting up—I can tell because his breathing sounds ragged and doggy. Rain starts drumming on my roof. I look at the ceiling, which seems to be sagging in on itself. It's not my ceiling, so let it crumble.

"I miss you at lunch," I say.

"The world is your oyster," he says. He said the same words when I told him my period was late, very late and that we had a pink color from it all. Still, he said, he was moving to London to help raise his elementary school kids. The main thing, he told me, was that his brother would never fire me—that I was like family. As long as I remained with the firm. His voice sounded thick, like he'd just received Novocain.

"So we're a firmly?" I'd said, blood warming up my face like a space heater that really worked.

He didn't laugh. He never laughs.

On the phone there are silences and delays—words that could have been taken from flash cards. My voice echoes back at me, and I hate the sound of it. I imagine the glow of his cigarette illuminating London. I hang up and it all comes out. After I clean my mouth and face, I take a walk.

The Madonna Round Evelina's

Pierre J. Mejlak

H E HAD MET her at the Hungry Duck, in the heart of Moscow, where the ladies can drink as much as they like free of charge until half eleven at night. The two of them happened to be at the bar. She with a Hanky-Panky, he a Vodka Martini. Their eyes fell first on the glasses; then, they looked at each other and realized that they were, kind of, alone. And it's astonishing how, even in the freeze of Moscow, one word leads to another.

And six months later there she was, with him in the house he inherited from his grandfather, in a small village in a dwarfish country somewhere between Sicily and Libya. Roża—the neighbor across the road, who administered the holy communion to the old ladies of the village—said that in order to find a woman he must have bought her. Others elaborated somewhat and said that he bought her over the Internet. And there were some who would smile whenever they saw the couple, as if they were some kind of joke. Of course, some of the priests and those a little too intimate with them would look at the couple as if they were seeing

Judas Iscariot carrying a crate of Hopleaf beer. Because— quite obviously—they were living in sin.

They were happy. She took care of the house, decorated it, watered the bougainvillea, killed the flies and rode around on her bicycle, whilst he would shuttle home from work and to work from home. They never spoke much about religion, except for the obvious stuff, such as "see that over there, look, that's a church" or almost in passing, like when she took down a poster of the Last Supper from the kitchen wall because it didn't match the decoration, and he accepted with a hug. He was a Catholic. Baptised, first communion and confirmation. But as Evelina never mentioned mass or anything along those lines, he didn't want to bring them up himself. Until one day, a Saturday morning, whilst Evelina was out on her bike, they brought them the Madonna.

"We brought you the Madonna," said the neighbor, as he opened the front door.

The Madonna was passed around the entire village, from one end to the other, each house passing her to the next. Each home would keep her for two days, mostly in the kitchen with the oil from the chip pan slapping her face, or in the sitting room next to Super One TV.

What was he to do? Tell the neighbor he didn't want it because it didn't match Evelina's decoration? Refuse the Madonna? Wasn't it to her that he prayed whenever he was in the doctor's waiting room squirming with pain? And now he should refuse her? No chance. He took her inside, placed her on the kitchen table, and went back to cutting his toenails. Then, in came Evelina.

"What the hell is that?"

"What you want it to be, Evelina, ħi? That's the Madonna."

"And what is the Madonna doing in our kitchen?"

It was useless trying to explain what it was all about. There was no point in showing her there were people who kept their lives occupied in these things. Evelina took the Madonna and put her under the stairs, such that you had to crouch down in order to see her, as if having to go under a truck.

"The Madonna can stay there for these two days."

And he did as usual. He remained silent. Unnecessary arguments annoyed him. But that evening, in the house named "In-Nann" (after his grandfather), strange things began to occur. First the lights went out. Theirs only in the entire street. And as soon as he tried to flick the circuit breaker, it spat out a flame which very nearly roasted his hand. It was too late to call Ġużi the electrician, so they decided that just for that night they would go to bed early. And, with a slowly smoldering candle on either side of the queen-size bed, he lay down and began to stare at the ceiling, and at the strange shadows forming before his eyes. Amidst them, a large shadow began to take shape. It was the form of an arrow. No, actually, it was more like a Christmas tree. No. And then, clear as crystal, a woman appeared . . . with a veil. The Madonna under the stairs! Then began the nightmares. The fires of hell. The screaming. The chains. The sobbing. The devils and who knows what else.

The following day, when Evelina came in from her bike ride, she was greeted by the statuette of the Madonna on the commode at the front of the house.

"What the fuck is this?"

That day, for the first time, they quarreled fiercely.

Translated by Antoine Cassar

My Brother at the Canadian Border

Sholeh Wolpé

FOR OMID

O N THEIR WAY to Canada in a red Mazda, my brother and his friend, Ph.D.s and little sense, stopped at the border and the guard leaned forward, asked: Where you boys heading? My brother, Welcome to Canada poster in his eyes, replied: Mexico. The guard blinked, stepped back then forward, said: Sir, this is the Canadian border. My brother turned to his friend, grabbed the map from his hands, slammed it on his shaved head. You stupid idiot, he yelled, you've been holding the map upside down.

In the interrogation room full of metal desks and chairs with wheels that squeaked and fluorescent light humming, bombarded with questions, and finally: Race? Stymied, my brother confessed: I really don't know, my parents never said, and the woman behind the desk widened her blue eyes to take in my brother's olive skin, hazel eyes, the blonde fur that covered his arms and legs. Disappearing behind a plastic partition, she returned with a dusty book, thick as *War and Peace*, said: This will tell us your race. Where was your father born? she asked, putting on her horn-rimmed glasses. Persia, he said. Do you mean I-ran?

Iran, you ran, we all ran, he smiled. Where's your mother from? Voice cold as a gun. Russia, he replied. She put one finger on a word above a chart in the book, the other on a word at the bottom of the page, brought them together looking like a mad mathematician bent on solving the crimes of zero times zero divided by one. Her fingers stopped on a word. Declared: You are white.

My brother stumbled back, a hand on his chest, eyes wide, mouth in an O as in O my God! All these years and I did not know. Then to the room, to the woman and the guards: I am white. I can go anywhere. Do anything. I can go to Canada and pretend it's Mexico. At last, I am white and you have no reason to keep me here.

Skull of a Sheep

James Claffey

YOU ARE IN a car speeding through Dublin toward the West year after year the journey uncoils past the same landmarks Kilmainham Jail strapped to a chair bullet to the brain on by the Rowntree Mackintosh factory where the black and yellow and orange and red fruit gums and sugar-covered pastilles spit out of humming machines through the streets by the Deadman's Inn where in the last century the cellar was a makeshift mortuary for corpses carried in from stagecoaches and a little further up the road the Spa Hotel perched on a hillside like some angular magpie on a branch and out the road we whizz by the Hitching Post and the Salmon Leap Inn into the country the green sward dotted with black-and-white cows cudding the grass tripartite stomachs long-lashed eyes lulled creatures the spire of the church in Kinnegad visible well before driving into the narrow-streeted town and Da stopping to wet his whistle at Jack's Roadhouse and Eamonn's butcher's shop next door where we bought beef and lamb and turkey at Christmas and on toward the West through pastureland with the distillery and the castle and Da's cry of "Goodbye Ireland I'm off to Kilbeggan" and Horseleap aptly named as in a blink the town disappears and with it the hillside graveyard where our ancestors' bones lie and into Moate of the widest main street in Ireland site of our family's bitterest defeat at the hands of bank manager and solicitors aided and abetted by the Sisters of Mercy later reputed to be torturers and abusers in habits and all wringing hands and uttered prayers Hail Holy Queens and the family business on the right the long low building and Da's mutters of regret and Mam saying bad luck go with it and out past Morgan Lane the vet's house on the left and the sight of him with his bordissio ready to geld the lily-white testicles of young boys through tree-lined arbors into Athlone—Mam's town and the narrowed streets houses falling in on one another the Prince of Wales Hotel and across the road Uncle Tom's shop and the room where you remember seeing Granny in the bed the lights dimmed camphor and mothballs and the mutinous Shannon out the window at the bottom of the slipway and off across the river by Custume Barracks and Lough Ree where Mam as a small girl waited in the rushes for swans and salmon and Lecarrow and Castlerea until the day stretches toward evening and tired voices recite Hail Marys and Our Fathers and the Rosary beads clack in the stuffy car and Da berates Mam for not teaching us our prayers and is it heathens she's raising and the air of summer full of ire and Castlebar turns toward Westport and the Wild Animal Park we never visit disappears as the Atlantic coast gapes in front of us and Rosturk fades behind us and over the humpy bridge where Loftus the postman will take flight years later on his Honda fifty and wind up dead in a ditch the motorcycle bent in half six children fatherless and the cottage by the dirt road owned by people named Coughlan awaits us without television and the fields lead to the edge of the water and the place where you find the sheep's skull and Mam won't let you take it inside and it rots on the window ledge and beneath the thatched roof Swallows and Amazons and Famous Five and Hardy Boys mysteries mark the long days of summer until once more the Rowntree Mackintosh factory and Kilmainham Jail appear and Da declares there to be "no place like home."

Arm, Clean Off

Cate McGowan

THE IRRIGATION MACHINE took it, slashed his arm off, a thick gash and a click of bones as it sliced right through. He'd dropped the wrench, reached into the engine to retrieve it. His dad had always said not to, but who would know? No one was around.

He jabbed his hand in for the tool. But then the fan blades cut his left arm, clean off. Clean through. Just above the elbow.

He took a header off the top of the engine into the wet field, green clumps swallowing him up. Skeins of sweet-smelling alfalfa grass danced in rhythm to the pulsing hoses. As the irrigation machine spasmed water, grinding wheels rolled by, oblivious to the fourteen-year-old's crisis.

He licked the salty corners of his mouth, gazed up and saw crimson on the plants where he'd toppled. *Think through this, shape a plan. Other people have emergencies, everybody does. Everybody takes a look up at the sky and faces it sometime.* He thought of people in other places, lying in rocky soil, watching the same sky. Beautiful girls pouting in parks, kids homesick at camp. Flat on their backs.

The cut decided on a dull throb, which droned in tempo—

"one-and-two-and . . ." He grabbed at something sticky by his knee as he pushed up. It was his cut-off arm. He clutched it, then set it down gingerly.

"A tourniquet'll save your life, son," he remembered his dad once saying when they were watching a Western.

The belt came off easy, even with one arm. He held the leather in his teeth and lay down to wiggle his left stub through the loop, then grabbed and cinched the strap, gripped it with his incisors. Groping around, he found a thick twig and stuck it in the buckle, twisted and tightened it over his wound. He swiped his gooey red hand along the leg of his jeans.

Down the slope, he could see the family farmhouse. He was alone—he'd been left to work while they shopped in town. No one would hear him call. The field was empty even—only the fierce, excited din of birds and bugs calling from far off, the occasional bark of a dog at some distant farm. *Think through this, shape a plan.*

Two fields and a tree-stand away was the Potters' farm.

He'd walk. With his arm. The field was spinning with the irrigation. Water was in his boots now. The dark, rich soil made an oozing, bubbling sound as he stepped.

His cut-off arm was dead weight like a cradled football; he touched the dead fingers, so strange. One foot, then the other. He pushed ahead, water from the machine still trickling down his cheeks.

The day burst with changing light, and he walked in and out of cloud shadows. The mottled purple shade volleyed back and forth. Trees danced in the distance, and the grass parted, a groundhog zigzagging through it across the pasture.

Up past a clearing, he stumbled between two crabapple trees. A flurry of gnats swarmed his wound. The raw calls of crows—*CAW, CAW*—accused him.

Down the ravine, a few more steps. It was hard to see it. A few more steps. He twisted the tourniquet again.

In the stream, the bottle-green water trickled over pebbles and rocks. And then he was there.

Mrs. Potter appeared out of nowhere, an apron around her waist, her open mouth spinning in an orbit of orange lipstick as she hollered for her husband, for everybody. Mr. Potter came running.

"Here's my arm," was the first thing the boy said. He offered his severed limb like a package.

They fetched him up as if he was a hog-tied goat. Then Mrs. Potter was beside him on the porch, little glistening beads of sweat on her upper lip fur as she shakily held a glass for him.

The boy lay back, scanned past sparkling motes to a silhouette cutting its way across the yard; Mr. Potter loped to meet the ambulance, and his long shadow spread and opened like a pair of scissors.

The boy's gaze then went farther up where a cloud in the west formed a big hand, the forefinger pointing like that famous picture he'd seen of God and Adam. He knew he'd have to tell his parents, *Don't cry, Mom. Dad, you stop your crying.*

Finished Symphony

Augusto Monterroso

"AND I COULD tell you," the fat man interjected in a rush, "that three years ago in Guatemala an old organist in a neighborhood church told me that in 1929 when he was asked to catalogue the music manuscripts in La Merced he suddenly found some unusual pages that intrigued him and he began to study them with his usual devotion and because the notes in the margins were written in German it took him a long time to realize they were the two final movements of the *Unfinished Symphony* so I could just imagine his feelings when he saw Schubert's signature written clearly and when he ran out to the street in great excitement to tell everyone of his discovery they laughed and said he had lost his mind and wanted to trick them but since he was a master of his craft and knew with certainty that the last two movements were as excellent as the first two he did not lose heart but swore instead to devote the rest of his life to making people admit the validity of his discovery and that was why from then on he dedicated himself to methodically visiting every musician in Guatemala with such awful

results that after fighting with most of them and without
saying anything to anybody least of all his wife he sold his
house and went to Europe and once he was in Vienna it was
even worse because they said no Guatemalan *Leiermann** was
going to teach them how to find lost works least of all ones
by Schubert whose scholars were all over the city and how
could those pages have ended up so far from home until
almost desperate and with only enough money for his return
passage he met a family of elderly Jews who had lived in
Buenos Aires and spoke Spanish and listened to him very
attentively and became very agitated when God knows how
they played the two movements on their piano viola and vio-
lin and at last grew tired of examining the pages every which
way and smelling them and holding them up to the light that
came in through the window and finally found themselves
obliged to admit at first very quietly and then with great
shouts they're by Schubert! they're by Schubert! and began
to cry in despair on each other's shoulders as if instead of
finding the pages they had just lost them and I would have
been amazed at how they continued to cry although they
calmed down a little and after talking among themselves in
their own language tried to convince him as they rubbed
their hands together that the movements excellent as they
were added nothing to the value of the symphony just as it
was and on the contrary one could say they detracted from it
since people had grown used to the legend that Schubert tore
them up or did not even try to write them certain he would
never surpass or even equal the quality of the first two and
the pleasure lay in thinking if this is how the *allegro* and the
andante are what must the *scherzo* and the *allegro ma non troppo*
be like and if he really respected and revered the memory

---

* organ-grinder

of Schubert the most intelligent thing would be to allow
them to keep the music because besides the fact that there
would be an endless polemic the only one who would lose
anything would be Schubert and then convinced he could
never achieve anything among the philistines much less the
admirers of Schubert who were even worse he sailed back
to Guatemala and one night during the crossing under a full
moon shining against the foaming sides of the ship with the
deepest sadness and sick of fighting bad people and good he
took the manuscript and ripped the pages one by one and
threw the pieces overboard until he was certain that now no
one would ever find them again"—the fat man concluded
in a certain tone of affected melancholy—"while great tears
burned his cheeks and he thought bitterly that neither he nor
his country would ever claim the glory of having returned
to the world those pages that the world should have received
with so much joy but which the world with so much common sense had rejected."

Translated by Edith Grossman

When a Dollar Was a Big Deal

Ari Behn

H E LET HIS beard grow and traveled to America, read Arthur Rimbaud, and wrote poems. On the bus from New York to Los Angeles he met a girl who was on the run. The girl said the childcare people were after her. Her mother was a junkie and her stepfather hit her. He stroked her crotch. When she got off next morning in Knoxville she gave him her father's address. He stayed on the bus until late the next morning holding that little note in his hand. He flew home from Los Angeles after losing all his travel money in Las Vegas and hitchhiking across the Mojave Desert. Back in Norway he sent a letter to the girl who had got off the bus in Tennessee. "You're the best thing that ever happened to me," he wrote. "Maybe we belong together . . . ?" Three weeks later the letter came back. ADDRESS UNKNOWN was printed in capital letters across the envelope. The American postal service paid the return postage. This too was written in capital letters. As though a dollar was such a big deal.

Translated by Robert Ferguson

Amerika Street

Lili Potpara

I's been quiet in the apartment for a week with Daddy and Mama not talking. Today, they are both working and the girl has been alone, playing a game where she talks to herself, asking questions and answering them in a different voice. Mama comes home early and calls, "Alenka, come into the kitchen."

Alenka apologizes to her toys and tells them she'll be back quickly.

"Alenka, I have to tell you something," says Mama.

She has that look that scares Alenka, as if it were drawn on the wrong face.

"Daddy got you a birthday surprise," she says. "A bike. One of those Rog Pony folding bicycles."

Alenka doesn't say anything, but something makes her heart tighten, and she's angry. She'll be eleven years old soon, not a child anymore. Of course she wants a Pony. She's wanted a Pony for a long time, so that she can go with Silva and Katarina to "Amerika," a little side street. It's been too far away for her, without a bike. They talk so much about it, how the slopes are steep, and how you have to brake hard at the bottom, that she wishes that they'd talk about something else.

Mama continues with that look, the one drawn on the wrong face, "Alenka, you should look happy because Daddy even took out a loan to buy it."

She says, "Yes, Mama," and goes back to the window and her toys, "I'm going to get a bicycle as a surprise," she tells them, and the toys bounce up and down.

When her birthday arrives, Alenka has a tummy ache. Still, she goes to school, and in class she wonders whether the bike is red or blue. All the Ponies are blue or red, only Silva's is pink because her daddy painted it.

At home Daddy arrives after lunch and tells her to come down to the basement. Alenka goes down and the bike is there. Light blue.

She glances at her father. She knows that she's supposed to be happy, but her tummy starts to hurt more. She touches the bike. It's just right—the metal so cold it slightly hurts.

"Thank you, Daddy," she says and wants to go upstairs to her toys as soon as possible.

"You're not going to go for a ride?" he asks.

"Yeah," Alenka says, not knowing what to do. "In a little while."

The basement is narrow and the light is poor; Daddy is big and Alenka is small. She can't move. In her head, she hears the word "loan." She wishes Daddy would leave, so Silva and Katarina can come, so she can escape to Amerika.

Translated by Kristina Zdravič Reardon

Joke

Giannis Palavos

STAVROS LAID DOWN the screwdriver.

"Done," he said. "Come look."

Katerina came out of the kitchen wiping her hands on a towel.

"What's that?"

"An elevator sign."

Katernia looked at the words on the bathroom door:

"CAUTION: Before entering make sure the car is positioned behind the door and has come to a full stop."

"I found it this morning in the garbage," Stavros said. "I thought I'd hang it here as a joke."

Katerina shook her head. They'd been housemates for six months. But not once had she laughed at any of his jokes.

"I made some fries," she said. "Want to eat?"

Midway through spring semester, at the end of March, Stavros's father went to the hospital for tests. The results showed cancer of the liver—luckily at an early stage. Stavros went back to his village for a month and a half. His mother spent nights at the hospital while he took care of their newspaper stand. When he returned to Thessaloniki, he found a stranger in his room.

"This is Vicente," Katerina informed him. "He's staying with us for a while. Hope that's all right."

Vicente was a year older. He was an architecture student from Barcelona on an Erasmus exchange in Greece. He and Katerina had met at a concert at the University three weeks ago. They'd gotten together the next day.

When the Spanish guy went out for groceries, Katerina hugged Stavros. She told him how crazy she was about the architecture student. They had only two more months before he had to go back to Spain. Too bad they met so late. How would she live without him? She took a piggy bank from her bookcase and shook it. "I'm saving up," she said, "for my airfare in September."

Stavros unpacked his suitcase.

"How's your father?"

"Better, thanks."

When Vicente came back, he took his bag into Katerina's room. He was tactful. The apartment was small, and he felt bad that he was inconveniencing Stavros. When the two of them were at school, he'd cook up hot, colorful dishes—and then make sure the sink was sparkling clean. At night they'd all watch movies or sometimes sing karaoke together, something, he said, everyone did in Catalonia. They never fooled around when Stavros was in the house, or at least if that was happening, Stavros didn't pick up on it. They were so quiet. The guy even liked the elevator joke on the bathroom door. "Muy bien, Stavros," he said and slapped him on the back. The weeks passed, and there were moments when Stavros almost liked him, but only briefly, because he too was completely in love with Katerina, from the very first day they'd rented the apartment together.

Stavros didn't talk about relationships or his feelings. On the contrary, he comforted Katerina when she'd say she was scared of losing her new boyfriend. He'd go out with the couple, accompany them for a drink. The last Saturday, two days before the Spaniard had to leave, the three of them went on an outing to Lake Kerkini. Stavros drove, and Vicente was in the back clicking picture after picture of pelicans. They ate at a taverna owned by an uncle of Katerina's who used to be a volunteer for Doctors Without Borders in Malawi. The waiter brought the bill just when Vicente was telling Stavros how he was going to miss him. Stavros smiled as he looked for his wallet. "No, por favor," Vicente insisted, "invito yo. I owe you one."

Sunday evening they sat in the living room and shared a beer, a Kaiser. At first Katerina seemed calm, but then she began to cry. Vicente cried too. Stavros left them alone and took his beer to sweat it out on the balcony. It was 2 a.m. when the Spaniard gathered up his things, said good-bye to Stavros, and locked himself up with Katerina in her room. Stavros lay down and tried to sleep, but different stuff was going on in the room next door, crying at first, then moans. It was the first time he'd heard them in bed. When they'd finished, the crying started again, but this time it was more muffled. In the dark Stavros thought he smelled them breathing. He imagined them three feet away on the other side of the wall, his hand in her hair, hers on his chest. He wanted to vomit. He got up to pee, but when he opened the bathroom door, nothing was there.

Translated by Karen Van Dyck

Heavy Bones

Tania Hershman

"It's me bones," I say. "They're real heavy, I've always been like that. Honest, it's not you." But he just stands there looking all washed out. Only a few minutes ago, we were still tipsy from the bubbly at the reception, our heads fizzing, and now I'm standing here freezing on the doorstep in my big white dress and he's looking like he's failed his first big husbandly duty and what does that say about all the rest of it and why don't we just call it quits right now. I sigh real loudly, look up and down the street a bit, rubbing me arms warm, but he's just staring into space and looking like he might cry, my skinny new hubby, with all of him drained away.

Suddenly I know what to do. I grab him under the armpits and heave him over the doorway. "How's that, eh?" I say, puffing and sweating under all my frothy meringue. He's shocked, staring at me boggle-eyed. Then he grins and once he starts he don't stop grinning. "Not bad," he says, "not bad at all, wifey." And he plants a big one on me, right on me lips, with all the neighbors who think I don't know they're there, watching, going Oooh, look at that, bit cheeky, eh. He pulls me right in and slams the front door in all their nosy faces. "Last one to the bedroom's got heavy bones!" he shouts. I pick up my skirts and start running.

Dream #6

Naguib Mahfouz

THE TELEPHONE RANG and the voice at the other end said, "Shaykh Muharram, your teacher, speaking."

I answered politely with a reverent air, "My mentor is most welcome."

"I'm coming to visit you," he said.

"Looking forward to receiving you," I replied.

I felt not the slightest astonishment—though I had walked in his funeral procession some sixty years before. A host of indelible memories came back to me about my old instructor. I remembered his handsome face and his elegant clothes—and the extreme harshness with which he treated his pupils. The shaykh showed up with his lustrous jubba and caftan, and his spiraling turban, saying without prologue, "Over there, I have dwelt with many reciters of ancient verse, as well as experts on religion. After talking with them, I realized that some of the lessons I used to give you were in need of correction. I have written the corrections on this paper I have brought you."

Having said this, he laid a folder on the table, and left.

Translated by Raymond Stock

Daniela

Roberto Bolaño

M Y NAME IS Daniela de Montecristo and I am a citizen of the universe, although I was born in Buenos Aires, the capital of Argentina, in the year 1915, the youngest of three sisters. Later my father remarried and had a little son, but the child died before his first birthday, and Papa had to be happy with what he had, that is, with my sisters and me. I don't know why I'm explaining all this. It's ancient history, or children's stories if you like, of no interest to anyone now. I lost my virginity at the age of thirteen. That might interest someone. I was deflowered by one of the ranch hands. I can't remember his name, all I know is that he was a ranch hand and must have been somewhere between twenty-five and forty-five. He didn't rape me, I do remember that. At least I never thought of it as rape, afterward I mean, when it was over, and I was getting dressed behind an ombu tree, and the ranch hand, around the other side, was pensively rolling a cigarette, which he then lit and gave me for a couple of puffs on it, my first ever puffs of smoke. I remember that vividly. The bitter taste of

tobacco and the plains stretching away endlessly and my
legs trembling. What was really trembling, though, were
my thoughts. I could have gone and told on him. All night
I kept turning the idea over in my mind, and the next two
nights as well. But I didn't do it. Partly because I wanted to
repeat the experience. Partly because it wasn't my father's
ranch; it belonged to one of his friends, so the punishment
wouldn't have been administered by my blood relations, it
would have fallen outside what I took to be the ambit of
real justice, the justice of the blood. My father never had
a ranch. My older sister married a lawyer, a pathetic shy-
ster who never tired of declaring his inordinate love for my
father. My other sister married the son of a ranch owner, a
crazy kid who within a few years managed to gamble away
a small fortune and get himself cut out of the will. To sum
up: my family was always middle class, and whatever efforts
we made, from our various starting points, in our various
and often contradictory ways, to climb up a rung and enter
the rigid, immutable upper crust, official guardian of justice
and morality, the fact is we never moved out of our social
compartment, which, although comfortable, condemned
the livelier minds in the clan (myself, for example) to a restlessness that even then, at the age of thirteen, on that ranch,
which wasn't our property, I could glimpse like a dizzying
mirage, a space in time where time itself was cancelled,
time as we know it, and that was why I began by saying that
I am a citizen of the universe and not, as the saying goes, of
the world, because I may be old but it should be quite clear
that I'm not stupid, and the world cannot contain a dizzying
mirage like that, although perhaps the universe can. But I
was talking about restlessness. I was talking about the night
when I thought about telling on the ranch hand who had
deflowered me. I didn't, and I didn't have sex with him

again. Restlessness, my first apprehension of restlessness, declared itself as a fever, so my father sent me back to Buenos Aires, where I was entrusted to the care of a physician, Dr. Guarini.

Translated by Chris Andrews
with Natasha Wimmer

Sovetskoye Shampanskoye

Berit Ellingsen

0 IS WHOLENESS and emptiness at once. It is the crystal stars and the shivering path of the northern lights, blood from the sun that bursts in the atmosphere. The aurora spills green, blue, yellow, white across his retinas. The snow creaks under his stubby skis, pushed by his stubbier legs. He stumbles, having learned to walk just a year ago, but the ski poles catch him.

1 is a thin stream that trickles past birches and ferns and lady's mantle. The mud makes it difficult to walk and easy to fight. Here he learns the difference between his own needs and those of others. The officers throw the recruits a raw salmon. He grabs the scaly flesh, bites and swallows without chewing, tears again, before someone punches him in the gut, elbows him in the back, and takes the fish from him. He wipes his greasy fingers on a black-and-white trunk, rough bark nipping his skin.

2 are the bulbous, multicolored domes of the capital's cathedral that are not yet covered with snow when he arrives. White mutes long avenues, blanches red walls, and moistens

heavy coats. He doesn't appear native; Vilnius, his passport says. In a city of immigrants, nobody asks about Lithuania.

3 are the lace curtains that lift in the summer breeze as he moves in and out of the committee member's young, dark-haired assistant. She types 100 words a minute and comes from somewhere behind the Ural Mountains. He warms her body with his smile, as he does with everyone he meets. He smiles like everything happens for a reason.

4 is the number of glasses his wife, the former assistant to the committee member, now a member herself, places on the oval table to include the committee secretary and his spouse. Unfertilized sturgeon eggs from the muddy and tepid waters of the Black Sea, in a leaded crystal bowl with a wide-handled silver spoon, along with sparkling Belarusian Chardonnay—Sovetskoye Shampanskoye, Soviet champagne—chill the teak wood. In the light from the living room candles, the serving cart burns golden.

5 is the cold mirror of the Moskva River and the stripped trees in Gorky Park that watch a Western asset on a long-term visa be garroted in a doorway, documents and micro-films in his briefcase, the man's status exposed by a phone call. The gilded Regency doors of the newest central committee member's apartment vibrate loudly at 3 a.m. Her husband opens in his bathrobe. The security forces push past him and into the committee member's office. Under the tinkling light of the Czechoslovakian crystal chandelier in the hall ceiling, he presses his naked feet onto the checkered floor and doubles over.

6 are the white tiles he spatters when they ask about his wife's documents and microfilms, repeatedly and with closed fists. He doesn't lie, tells them about her late hours in the commit-

tee building, the meetings, the phone conversations. They apprehend her. Behind the gilded Regency doors, underneath the unlit crystal, he stands in silence while he considers the nature of truth. He takes up a new position in the city.

7 are the years that follow, when he gathers information like eiderdown. Years of wan smiles and cold handshakes, while ice shrouds and flays the Moskva River and clouds rush across the sky like time.

8 is the number of days it takes for the cosmos to entropy into chaos in the pewter sunlight off the river. Assets are lost, intentions blocked. They take him back to the white tiles and ask him again, this time more insistently. The information he transmitted was tailored to distract. Now he is no longer useful and his employer has been notified. He expects to be killed, desires it almost. Instead, they put him in a noisy plane and fly.

9 is the ammunition that bulges inside guns as he steps onto the steel of Glienicke Bridge. Will it come from the betrayed past or a preemptive future? The air smells of the West, fitful and variegated. When he reaches the midpoint of the water, he shifts his gaze to the person that passes him. He is surprised, although he knows he shouldn't be. The spring wind rustles long dark hair, replaying in him the taste of unfertilized sturgeon eggs from the warm waters of the Black Sea, and sparkling Belarusian Chardonnay.

Consuming the View

Luigi Malerba

THE SKY WAS clear and the air clean, yet from the telescopes on the Gianicolo hill the Roman panorama
appeared hazy and out of focus. The first protests came from
a group of Swiss tourists complaining that they had wasted
their hundred lire on malfunctioning devices. The city
sent out an expert technician, who had the lenses replaced.
Nonetheless, protests kept coming, in writing and by phone.
City Hall sent out another expert to test the telescopes again.
A peculiar new element emerged: the panorama from the
Gianicolo appeared blurry not only through the lenses of
the telescopes but also to the naked eye. The city claimed the
problem was no longer its responsibility, yet the tourists kept
complaining, in writing and by phone. After gazing for a
while at the expanse of rooftops, with the domes of Roman
churches surfacing here and there and the white monument
of the Piazza Venezia, many went to have their eyes checked.
Some even started wearing glasses.

A professor of panoramology was called in, from the
University of Minnesota at Minneapolis. She leaned over

the Gianicolo wall at varying hours: dawn, daybreak, noon, sunset, even at night. Finally she wrote a lengthy report on the distribution of hydrogen in the photosphere, on phenomena of refraction, on carbon dioxide polluting the atmosphere, and even on the fragrance given off by exotic plants in the Botanical Garden below—without recommending any remedy.

A doorman at City Hall, who lived near the Gianicolo and who had learned of the problem, wrote a letter to the mayor explaining a theory of his. According to the doorman, the Roman panorama was being slowly worn away by the continuous gaze of tourists, and if no action were taken it would soon be entirely used up. In a footnote at the end of his letter, the doorman added that the same thing was happening to Leonardo da Vinci's *Last Supper* and other famous paintings. In a second footnote he emphasized, as proof of his thesis, how the view visibly worsened in the spring and summer, coinciding with the great crowds of tourists, while in the winter, when tourists were scant, one noticed no change for the worse; on the contrary, it seemed the panorama slowly regained its traditional limpidity.

Other expert panoramologists took photographs from the Gianicolo week after week, and these seemed to confirm the doorman's theory. The truth, however strange, now seemed crystal clear: the constant gaze of tourists was consuming the Roman panorama; a subtle leprosy was slowly corroding the image of the so-called Eternal City.

The City Hall public relations office launched a campaign, which, in order to discourage tourists, tried to ridicule the panorama in general, the very concept of a view. Their press releases had titles like "Stay Clear of the Panorama" and "The Banality of a View." Others, more aggressive, were entitled "Spitting on the Panorama," "Enough of

This Panorama," "One Cannot Live on Views Alone." A famous semiologist wrote a long essay entitled "Panorama, Catastrophe of a Message." Some journalists abandoned themselves to malicious and gratuitous speculation on the greater corrosive power of Japanese or American or German tourists, according to their own whims or the antipathies of the newspapers in which the articles were published. Fierce discussions were unleashed, which, though noisy, achieved the opposite of the desired effect: all the publicity, though negative, ended up increasing the number of tourists crowding the Gianicolo hill.

Eventually, the Roman city government, following the advice of an expert brought in from China, resorted to the stealthy planting of a row of young cypresses under the Gianicolo wall, so that, within a few years, the famous panorama would be completely hidden behind a thick, evergreen barrier.

Translated by Lesley Riva

Reunion

Edward Mullany

JACK AND I were at the department store, and, as usual, Jack didn't want to be there, only this time he'd come with someone else.

I sat with him on the edge of one of those nice-looking beds. I'd been shopping all day, so in a way I was able to rationalize it.

From a nearby fitting room came the voice of a woman who evidently believed Jack was the only one who could hear her. We looked at each other with raised eyebrows. I knew who the woman was. But Jack and I had been divorced long enough to know that speaking of each other's mates when those mates weren't there to defend themselves inevitably led to suspicions of jealousy, even if what was said was meant to be funny, so we'd made it a rule to keep our mouths shut.

"You'd better go see what she wants," I said, and lifted one of my shopping bags in her direction.

Jack got up, but not before looking inside the bag. It was Christmas, and old habits die hard.

"What's going on?" said the woman from the fitting

room. She'd come out in a silk nightgown that looked better on her than it would have on me, but when she'd seen us she'd stopped, as if the sight of us together had made her forget why she was here.

"It's all right," said Jack. "You look great, sweetheart. Is that the one you want?"

The woman looked at me. Jack's hand was still in my shopping bag. He took it out slowly, like a child caught in the act of something insidious. I didn't say anything. But I did something I knew would communicate what I wanted to tell her, something that, even though I despised myself for it, I found myself unable to help. I smiled in a way that was suggestive rather than friendly, and arched just one of my eyebrows. The woman turned away in tears.

Later, when I met my husband in the mall, he tried to peek inside the shopping bag like Jack had done, but it wasn't the same, and I snapped at him.

The Interpreter for the Tribunal

Tony Eprile

WAS HIDING IN my friend's garage, a place no one would think to look. I had my informants, you see. We were boys together and I knew he'd never betray me. I waited until the time they usually brought him food and when he opened the door to my whistle, I was on him like a pack of wild dogs. He ground my face into the concrete, shouting horribly in my ear. The pain was terrible. I did not know what was happening. The trick is to disorient the prisoner right away. Get him off guard and he'll tell you anything you want to know. My arm was twisted behind my back and I could feel the ligaments tearing. I did not struggle but he kept twisting, his knee my knee in his back you bastard you're done now he screamed I was thrust from the darkness into the light, then into the darkness again like a sack of potatoes I threw him into the trunk of my car, I'm that strong. I could hear him thumping in the trunk as I drove and hit the brakes taking the corners hard I bashed my head against something hard and was thrown helplessly into the light of a two-thousand-candlepower torch right in the eyes hitting him all the time the fists coming from nowhere and I felt a rib breaking, my nose breaking. The blood ran down his face and he didn't even lift a finger to wipe it off my glasses had come off when they got me and I had no idea where I was on the ground of that hut, and yes I sat on his back and pulled the sack over his head, the wet sack like I was drowning I could not breathe. He could not breathe, I pulled it off now you will tell me what I want to know because otherwise I could not breathe I told him everything it did not take long to get the names my friends who betrayed me the friends I did not know what I was saying what he was saying those were hard times and we had to be hard to live in them I just wanted the pain to stop but I have to live with who I am now who was I then it is too terrible to speak of it at all is to go mad.

The Gutter

Ethel Rohan

H<small>E ARRIVED HOME</small> from school and slipped into the dead feeling. As usual, the hallway was littered with purple Post-its, so old they'd lost their stickiness. The first of his mother's notes read "EAT," followed by others with inked arrowheads that pointed to the kitchen.

On the fridge, a new note read "Milk's off, only good for tea." On the stove, the usual note in red marker, "Don't touch." He sat at the kitchen table, and lined up crackers and the jar of peanut butter. He moved aside the note on the napkin holder that read "After snack, homework."

In the living room, the yellow Post-it on the TV screen read "Don't you dare." In his bedroom, on his desk, she'd written on a ruled sheet of yellow paper, "Check your homework, <u>twice</u>." On his DS game, "Only if you've done everything else." In the bathroom, on the toilet, her faded scribbles, "Flush. Wash Hands." Stuck to the front of the soap dish, "Count to 2̶5̶ 50. Slowly!"

On her bedroom door, "Stay Out." His father had walked out on his mother when she was pregnant, hadn't even waited to see what she'd given him. Lately, she'd taken to calling the boy the *man of the house*. Under his bedcovers, pinned to his flattened Paddington Bear, another new note, "Toss."

He returned to his mother's bedroom door, sniffed at its cracks and inhaled the traces of her face powder and spicy perfume. At six o'clock, when he heard her car pull into the driveway, he reached for the stack of orange Post-its.

He waited inside the front door, Paddington Bear clutched to his stomach. His mother stopped short. He had stuck the Post-it to his forehead. "Free—Please Take."

He pushed out past her, and took up his position on the street.

Three-Second Angels

Judd Hampton

THE CANYON JUMPERS reject your currency. They speak a progressive language, a language you mistrust and fear. The boys come dressed in deep baggy jeans, pre-soiled and studded for your displeasure. The girls reveal too much stomach, various degrees of chub, bellybutton ornaments, and jeans too low-cut for safety. The boys experiment with toothpicks wedged between their teeth. The girls snap ultra-cool-mint gum.

The canyon jumpers already know your ways to fall. They have their own ways. You suspect their ways are suspect.

They come after class, feet clapping the pavement with exaggerated goose steps they learned from twentieth-century history films. Cars pass them leaving wide berths. The canyon jumpers have nothing to say so they speak the words they hear at home.

They come with unexpected names. Keshtin, Bradleshaw and Wristen. Cholena, Marisitomia and Pirthenily. No Jacks and Jills go up these hills anymore. It is as if their parents named them expecting their angels to take flight.

Before reality was realized. Before expectations expired. Their mothers scrub toilets. Their fathers smell of gasoline.

"Why bother?"

"Why try?"

"Who cares?"

These are just words they speak at home.

"You're selfish."

"You're a disappointment."

"You're a goddamn waste."

These are just words they hear at home.

The canyon jumpers elbow through tour groups whose pullovers and heavy backpacks smack of gift shop ambush. The tourists speak a language of mediocrity the canyon jumpers abhor.

The canyon is their religion, a spiritual thing. The tourists are infidels. The canyon jumpers worship in endless pews of spruce and Douglas fir, a steeple of blue sky and sunlight, the rising spray from the canyon like a moist halo. They follow a footpath to emerald-green holy water and they anoint themselves. And then they climb.

When they reach the overhanging ledge, they bow their heads in reverence. "Remember Avery," one of them says. "Remember Charlene." In turn they step to the edge and spit. Fifty feet. One hunded feet. What does the drop matter?

They are quiet. Anxious. Fear is involved. The girls embrace the boys.

"Tighter, I can't feel you," one says.

"Well, you know—" says another.

"I wish. I wish. I wish."

These are just words they speak.

The canyon jumpers have learned to hold no faith in expectation. "See you at the bottom," they say, for luck. And then they soar. They fly like angels. Three seconds.

Three seconds to undo.

The Lament of Hester Muponda

Petina Gappah

AFTER HESTER MUPONDA lost her first child and she turned her face to the heavens to pour out her grief, her church people said to her, find your strength in God, they said to her. After the second child followed where the first had led, she bent her face into the folds of her Zambia wrapping cloth. The Lord gives and He takes away, blessed be His name today, Hester Muponda said. But when the fifth followed the fourth who had followed the third, she kept him in her second bedroom until he began to decay and smell and they forced the door open and still she refused to bury him. Her closest neighbor and best friend Mai-Ngwerume whispered something about Hester Muponda's midnight ways to her closest neighbor and best friend Mai-Mutero and MaiMutero said to MaiNgwerume, it is a mad chicken that eats its own eggs, but shush now.

He does not give us more than we can bear, Hester Muponda's church people said to her, look to your grand-children, they need you now, they said to her. Then first, the first grandchild died and then second, the second and Hester closed her bedroom door against her husband. And when Hester Muponda opened the door again, it was to show a beard on the chin of her disappearing face.

Only women with evil tempers grow beards, her husband's paternal aunts said. Hester Muponda's husband woke up in the night and reaching across the pillows, brushed his hand across her chin. He moved to the spare bedroom, and the day after the memorial service of the first dead grandchild, he moved out of the house and Ashdown Park altogether and moved in with Gertrude Chinake his woman from Bluff Hill who had no beard or grief but smelt only of sweat and sex and the Takatala sauce in which she marinated all their food.

Hester Muponda took up her large pots, her black pots she took up, her funeral pots in which had been cooked the meals that fed the mourners that cried her children and grandchildren away. She took up her pots and set up three three-stone fires at the corner of Eves Crescent and Ashdown Drive next to Gift Chauke who sold individual cigarettes and sweets and belts with shiny buckles and the *Financial Gazette* on Thursdays, the *Independent* on Fridays, and the *Herald* on every other day but Sunday when he sold the *Standard* and the *Sunday Mail*. In her pots she made sadza, thick and white, and chicken stew and vegetables that she sold to Gift Chauke and to the drivers and to the conductors of commuter omnibuses. And even though her cooking smells reached into the neighboring houses along with her pain, Edgar Jones the only white person left in Ashdown Park did not complain about property values as he had when his neighbors first started to grow maize in gardens meant for flowers and to park the heads of long-distance haulage trucks on the narrow strips of lawn outside their houses.

She is mad, Hester Muponda's neighbors said and crossed

the street when they saw her coming. Mad, mad, echoed the drivers and conductors and Gift Chauke as their teeth tore into the chicken that Hester Muponda cooked with onions and tomatoes. And when the time came, and Hester Muponda took up the blanket that covered her in the darkness that her children had found, the only people who felt her absence were those drivers and conductors who missed the firm but soft sadza and the chicken stew that Hester Muponda cooked over three three-stone fires at the corner of Ashdown Drive.

Farewell, I Love You, and Goodbye

James Tate

OUR LIVES GO on. Our fathers die. Our daughters run away. Our wives leave us. And still we go on. Occasionally we are forced (or so we like to say) to sell everything and move on, start over. We are fond of this mainly because we have so few left. The Starting-Over-God is, of course, as arbitrary as the one who took father before his time. But we have to hang onto something. So we start over. There is a little excitement to spice the enormous dread. Not again, I can't, I don't have it in me. I've seen this one before and I can't sit through it again. But we do, just in case. In case we missed some tiny but delicious detail all the other times we saw it.

Can you recommend a dentist, a doctor, an accountant, a reliable real estate agent, a bank? And before you know it, a life is beginning to fall into place. You have located the best dry cleaner, the best Chinese food. A couple of the shop owners have remembered your name. How long have you been here? they ask. And here is the opening, the opportunity you've been waiting for.

"I was born here," you reply, "lived here all my life."

Rooms full of pain, lawns of remorse, avenues of regret, whole shopping malls of grief begin to detach themselves from you, from the person, from this husk, this shell you call simply Bill.

"My name's Bill, I live just down the street, it's funny we haven't met before."

"Nice to meet you Bill. My name's Carla. I just opened the shop a week ago. I moved here from Chicago last summer. Divorce, you know."

She was an attractive woman, slight, fine-boned, and had a pleasant manner, and Bill couldn't imagine why anyone . . . He stopped himself. Let it go, let her previous life go. And why had he lied to her automatically? He wanted to clear it up right away, but what would she think, telling lies to a stranger, what kind of behavior is that, anyway?

"Carla, I have to apologize to you."

"Why? I don't understand."

"I haven't lived here all my life. I'm new in town. I just . . ."

"That's all right, you don't have to say anything."

"Well, then, can I buy you a drink or something when you close up today or some other day?"

"That'd be nice. Can you come by about five past five?"

"Great." And so it was starting again. Some single-minded agent of life was stirring, was raising its perky head, and Bill smiled and waved goodbye to Carla.

On the short walk back to his house Bill found himself humming an old Billie Holiday tune, "God Bless the Child that's got his own," and he laughed at himself and shook his head. Here he was in his new place, his new life, so much blood and ashes under the bridge. But it wasn't under the bridge. It was *his*, all that pain was not washed away, it was his, and suddenly he was proud of that. *Carla*, he said the name several times out loud. *Carla*, wow, who would have thought.

The Most Beautiful Girl

Peter Stamm

AFTER FIVE MILD, sunny days on the island, clouds started to mass. It rained overnight, and the next morning it was twenty degrees colder. I walked over the reef, a giant sandbar in the southwest, which was no longer land and not yet sea. I couldn't see where the water began, but I thought I had a sense of the curvature of the earth. Sometimes I crossed the tracks of another walker, though there was no one to be seen far and wide. Only occasionally a heap of seaweed, or a black wooden post corroded by seawater, sticking out of the ground. Somewhere I came upon some writing that someone had stamped in the wet sand with his bare feet. I followed the script, and read the word "ALIEN." In the distance I could hear the ferry, which was due to dock in half an hour. It was as though I could hear its monotonous vibration with my whole body. And then it began to rain, a light and invisible shower that wrapped itself around me like a cloud. I turned and walked back.

I was the only guest staying at the pension. Wyb Jan was sitting in the lobby with Anneke, his girlfriend, drinking tea. The room was full of model ships, Wyb Jan's father had been a sea captain. Anneke asked me if I wanted a cup of tea. I told them about the writing on the sand.

"Alien," I said. "It's exactly how I felt on that sandspit. As strange as if the earth had thrown me off." Wyb Jan laughed, and Anneke said: "Alien is a girl's name in Dutch. Alien Post is the most beautiful girl on the island."

"You're the most beautiful girl on the island," Wybjan said to Anneke, and kissed her. Then he tapped me on the shoulder and said: "When the weather's like this, it's best to stay indoors. If you go out, it might drive you crazy."

He went into the kitchen to get me a cup. When he came back, he switched on a lamp and said: "I'll put an electric heater in your room."

Anneke said: "I wonder who wrote that. Do you think Alien's found herself a boyfriend at long last?"

Translated by Michael Hoffman

The Ache

Elena Bossi

L ETHARGIC, LOOKING WITHOUT looking out the window of his fourth-story office, he longs for an adventure that would take him away from this place that has become unbearable.

This afternoon a boy is cleaning the big windows down on the street front. Whitish froth sprays out from the glass and spreads across the pavement, the way the pain in his shoulder does; it travels through his vertebrae to his feet, which are flattened by the weight he's accumulated over recent years. "Go to the doctor," his wife reproaches him. "Walk every day, eat less, and most of all, rest. Don't work so much." But if he stops working even for a moment, the pain is there. He doesn't really know where it comes from or even where it hurts. He wonders if its deep source is his conscience, his back, or his neck because in the end they might be the same thing. For years now his head and shoulders have seemed frozen into one block, which also makes it hard to distinguish mind from body.

The boy is cleaning the windows with frank, confident

sweeps, putting joy into each one. This work is pleasure to him; but not so absorbing that he doesn't check every moment up and down the street. He's expecting someone.

The man recalls the tenderness of his love for his wife and the constant desire that used to go with it, so fierce it was like a pain in the center of his being. It was a marvelous, indecent pain, which gave him no respite. That desire which he thought would last forever has dwindled, like a big catch cooked on a slow fire. Where did it go, that paradise of lips, teeth and tongue? Now kisses are avoided whenever possible; it is in the lips and tongue that love begins to spoil, where distance makes itself apparent.

He thinks that he wouldn't be able to live without her, that he owes her his life and everything he has. Gratitude and who knows how many other tangled sentiments have taken the place of passion. Indecency has been replaced by respect. He only wishes that his lips would lose their lush appearance and settle rather into the smile of a man who has realized all his plans.

Each night he finds a different excuse not to go to bed with her, or not at the same time, because what is the body's surrender without desire? It's well known that in the dark bodies seek and open to one another, revealing and discovering the secret that terrifies them.

And then down on the street it happens as he knew it would: the dark-haired girl coming along, so young, her skin alive, breasts brimming; it's all coming up at him from the street, emanating from these two. She is the one the window-cleaning boy is waiting to embrace.

The man just wants to see them together, to see the moment when the boy takes her about her waist, when she puts her arms around her lover's shoulders, to know from them the forgotten happiness; and maybe a caress will fly off and make its way to his own back and heal, at least for a moment, this ache. But the umbrella that is opening suddenly breaks the line of his gaze; it doesn't matter, he can move left and when the man with the umbrella passes, he'll be able to see the embrace anyway, or just after the crucial moment, but both of them will still be there. Except that now another umbrella is opening, and another, and the rain is not about to let up, and of course with this wet and all these umbrellas his back will go on aching.

Translated by Penelope Todd
and Georgia Birnie

The Young Widow

Petronius

A YOUNG WOMAN IN Ephesus was famous around town for being faithful to her husband. How sad when he died! It was only expected in the funeral procession that her hair would be tangled and she would wail and beat her naked breast before the crowd. Yet many were surprised when she even followed her husband's body down into the tomb. For days she continued to weep and tear her hair over him. No one could drag her away, not her parents, not the city officials, who were worried she would starve. But what could they do? Finally they left her with only her favorite slave-woman, who stayed by her side and refilled the lamp whenever it dimmed.

Meantime, the governor of the province ordered robbers to be crucified nearby. A soldier was posted to guard against families stealing any of the bodies to give them a proper burial. On the very first night he saw a light among the tombs and heard weeping; curious, he approached, looked into the vault, and was shocked to see a beautiful woman, like an apparition from the underworld. Then he saw her tears, her face gouged by her nails, and the corpse beside her, and understood—she was simply a young woman devastated by the loss of her husband. Moved, he brought his own supper into the tomb and offered it to her. It's no good to starve yourself, he said, gently consoling her. You must live, what good is sorrow? Don't we all come to the same end? The young woman only groaned, but the soldier did not retreat. Finally it was the slave-woman who put out her hand. She was famished, and grateful. As the food and wine began to restore her, she took the soldier's side. She begged her mistress, Why end your own life before fate demands it? Do you think the dead hear your cries? If he could, your husband would tell you to live.

At last the young widow gave in. It was like a fever breaking. She ate and drank and allowed herself to be taken into the soldier's comforting arms. It was clear how attracted they were to each other, and no surprise, since the soldier was young and handsome. The slave-woman smiled and started to leave them, but the young widow looked up, uneasy, so she sat by her mistress again and whispered, Let him console you. What's the harm? Will you fight even the healing powers of love?

You see where the story is going—why delay it? The widow and soldier lay together that night, and the next day and the next, keeping the doors of the vault shut, so anyone who came by would think the famously faithful wife had already breathed her last over her husband's corpse. As darkness fell each night the soldier slipped out and brought food and drink back to the tomb. As it happened, on the third night, the family of one of the crucified robbers saw the soldier had abandoned his post and they took the body down to give it last rites. Early the next morning the soldier saw the empty cross and knew what his fate would be. It was

far better not to wait for the judge's sentence but to die by
his own sword. He explained this to the young widow and
asked only that she give his body a place in the tomb with
her husband. May the gods forbid, she said, that I look at
the same time on the corpses of two men I love. Better to
make a dead man useful than send a living man to his death.
Then she ordered that her husband's body be taken out of
the tomb and fixed upon the empty cross. The soldier was
saved, since no one was the wiser, although eventually some
of the townspeople recognized the dead man and wondered
how he had ascended the cross.

Fun House

Robert Scotellaro

SHE'D GOTTEN THE fun house mirrors at an auction and had them put up in the spare bedroom. He found them strange, even a little disturbing, and thought the buy extravagant with the kids away at college and the big tuition bucks spilling out. But she'd insisted on a "well-deserved splurge" after all that *straight and narrow*. A side of her, new to him.

So he went along. Even following her one night, with a bottle of Marqués de Riscal, into that room with the lights dimmed and candles she placed on both dressers, adding to the mix. In bed, she began taking off her clothes, then his. "No way," he said, draining the last of the wine, gazing into one of the mirrors overhead, at their stretched-out, undulating forms; fleshy waves of them in the sheets.

He started to sit up, but she pulled him back. "This is weird, Connie," he said.

She reached out a zigzaggy hand and ran it down his zigzaggy middle. Looking left, she was squat and condensed, her cheeks bulged as if she had two apples stuffed in her mouth—her breasts large, wobbly globes. She guided his hand to them.

In another, the two of them were amoeboid, transforming silvery strangers. "You've got to be kidding me," he said. She smiled. And at a glance it was an astonishingly wide curl, liquid as mercury. He continued shifting his vision.

"My God!" he said.

"What?"

"The size of that thing."

She leaned over and whispered something. A name, he thought—not his own. Perhaps an endearment. She shook out her hair—jagged bolts against his chest. He closed his eyes, and when he opened them, she was wriggly and rosy. A stick figure, a block, a fleshy smear—strange and elegant. He heard some low, guttural sounds—his own.

She bit his shoulder and he pulled her close. His eyes banged against each corner of their sockets. The room was cluttered. It was ablaze with candlelight—squat fiery balls, elongated licks of light, and all their odd and flagrant infidelities in every piece of glass.

Squeegee

James Norcliffe

SQUEEZE THE MOP. I push the squeegee. The fine oil of humanity shines and rainbows on the tiles. I push the squeegee. All slides and slithers before me in a broad detergent smile, in a swathe of suds and scurf and tired bubbles. I squeeze the mop. I squeeze the mop's wet afro into the maw of the bucket. I push the squeegee. Sweet-scented steam clams on my brow. The mop's damp dreadlocks flip and flop. Body hairs curl, they shine like little springs of brightness, like crescents of bantam feathers. I push the squeegee. Bantams run before me in a frightened eccentric scatter. Behind them, behind the squeegee all is shiny, new. Before me sweat puddles and puddles, stains and stains. Behind me gloss glimmers. Hopes skitter before me with bright eyes, with frightened little feet. I push the squeegee. I squeeze the mop. I press the treadle and squeeze the mop. I move the bucket. Silence. Wide empty boulevards and broad leafy suburbs behind me. Quietude, the beatitude of sheen, shimmer and shine. Mess before me. Shambles, seepage and dreams. I push the squeegee. Squeezed foam filtered and flecked like wet feathers flows before me. I hear the cries of birds, the squeak and scrape of black rubber on shiny tiles. The scatter and fear. Blood flows before me red-feathered red and bubbly. I squeeze the mop. I move the bucket. I push. I push the squeegee.

CHINA

From the Roaches' Perspective

Qiu Xiaolong

AROUND TWO, WE begin to shudder underneath your tossing, turning over in the massage bed. Still dazed, hardly capable of thinking in coherence, your body sore, your legs weak, you stare into the darkness. What a day and night! Apart from four foot-washing customers outside, you had three other massage customers inside, particularly tough with the last one. An acquaintance of the salon owner with connections both in the black and white ways, he rams into you nonstop for hours, both from the front and from the behind. Afterward, he stays on, sprawling on the massage bed, apparently for the night rather than for a quickie as you have hoped. Covered in cold sweat, you feel as if numerous insects were crawling over your naked body.

"Cockroaches!" you curse between your clinched teeth, rising to massacre us.

We stampede in the terror of the night.

You grope down, marching barefoot through the curtain into the kitchen area, grasping the plastic slippers. Sure enough, you detect us rushing everywhere for shelters in the moonlight slashing through the back window. You start seeking us above the spill of moldering bowls and pots in the sink, chasing us among the bottles and jars of soy sauce, oyster oil, and fermented bean curd in the shelf above, driving us out of the rice bag. Then kneeling by the sink, as if in prayer, you launch an intensified search over the floor littered with our bodies, your thighs and legs dazzling through your unbelted nylon robe, still reeking of sex.

The scarlet slippers in your hands swooping down, jumping the chopsticks up into crosses, wreaking all of your fury at us, you pounce over to grind our bodies under your soft, round toes. Flashing against the bare wall, your black hair turns the dark night into delirious memories of the human refugees fleeing from the disastrous mudslide devouring your home village under the shadow of the Three Gorges Dam, all the trees and weeds removed from the hills and dales like your shaven armpits, all the paths turning into puddles with days drowning like bugs . . .

O God!

The light on, we see the man taking you from behind on the floor, savagely, just like one of us.

Not Far from the Tree

Karina M. Szczurek

Too tight. Strapped round her throbbing head, the
swimming goggles leave oval marks on the flesh around
her eyes. Underwater, with every stroke, arms stretched out,
palms cupped, willowy fingers pressed firmly together, she
focuses on the wedding band on her left ring finger, dis-
tinctly golden in the aquamarine translucence in front of
her. Underneath, the skin pale, indented like a chained oak.
Otherwise her hands olive-tanned; nails short, moon-skirted.

Like all women back home, her mother had worn hers
on the right hand for nearly thirty years. According to cus-
tom only widows change to left, she'd liked to remind her
daughter after Madolyn married a foreigner. And then, she'd
switched the sides herself to manifest a silent protest. Not
against death, but the crueler form of bereavement: an affair.

Madolyn had understood. Her father, in love, again. Her
mother unable to accept her part of the responsibility; left
alone, bitter: "One day, Maddy, you'll know too—I don't
wish it on you, but you'll see. They're all the same."

Froglike, her feet come together, sole to sole, as she slides through the lukewarm blueness of the pool. The sun rises reluctantly into the sweltering sky above their empty house; her husband away on business.

"Grass widow," her best friend had said last night at the party, pointing accusingly at her wedding ring. "If it wasn't for that, one wouldn't know you're married. We hardly ever see him." Madolyn's hand around another freshly mixed piña colada, the ring clinking against the icy glass.

"Could somebody take me home? I had one too many." She'd put the cocktail down on the yellowwood table next to her, readjusting the strap of her linen dress which had slipped off her shoulder.

Madolyn had got in behind the driver, his eyes watching her carefully in the rearview mirror. Crystal blue, she'd noticed in the light of the front passenger door opening to drop one other party guest somewhere along the way. Their eyes had locked a split second too long before she'd turned her head sideways and asked him not to take her home.

Family

Jensen Beach

SOMEONE SUGGESTED SWIMMING and someone else said that in this weather all we need is another incident. Someone recalled that there was an expression that perfectly explained this very moment. Someone said that yes they remembered it, lightning doesn't strike twice, and someone else said that as a matter of fact that's happened to a friend. Someone said that no one believed this story the first time and why should they all believe it now. Someone said that they'd read an article on the Internet about this topic and someone else said that, well then of course it's true. Someone suggested that everyone just calm down immediately. Someone began to walk away and someone reached out an arm to stop someone. Someone turned and said that they begged someone's pardon, but could they please release their grip. Someone struggled to hold on until someone else suggested that maybe lunch should be served, which turned the subject to food, which as usual had a calming effect. Someone prepared lunch and someone else set the table. Someone opened a bottle of wine and someone else accused someone

of drinking too much. Someone lifted a phone to call someone about this and someone said, could you please put the
phone down, lunch is served. Someone sat near the kitchen
so as to fetch items from the stove and to refill serving dishes
as necessary. Someone made a comment about someone's
cooking and someone else found this indulgent, and someone else found it simply untrue. Someone said that it was
raining now. Someone left the table and then the house until
someone was in the yard and looking up at the rain, and the
storm was large and billowing in the distance and the rain
was still light above the house and in the yard as it rained on
someone there. Someone pointed to the approaching storm
and someone else remarked at how dark it had suddenly
become. Someone said that someone had better be careful
out there and someone else pointed to the clouds, now thick
and black and seeming in some way to breathe if such a thing
is possible, and the rain fell in enormous drops and someone
started to run for cover. Someone saw a flash of lightning and
someone else said that, yes we all saw it. Someone no longer appeared to be in the yard and someone remarked upon
this change and someone else looked intently and rapidly at
every part of the yard visible from behind the large window,
which was now streaked with water. Someone else ran to the
kitchen for a similar, but slightly enlarged, view of the yard.
Someone sat still and hoped that someone was uninjured
and someone else attempted to determine the likelihood of
real life violating our most tested truths in this way, and as
someone sat and considered this question someone seemed
to recall that the expression someone had previously mentioned further qualified the circumstances of two lightning
strikes with location. Someone said out loud that this was a
variable someone had very foolishly forgotten and someone
else said that that was no big surprise. Someone else said,

what do you mean by that? Someone said that as a family we're always forgetting important details, and someone else said, do you mean forgetting or ignoring? Someone said to look out the window and someone else did, where they saw that someone was now lying on the grass near the house in a wet heap of someone. Someone said, did it happen? Someone said that it had and someone else said that it hadn't, and they all gathered there before the window in the kitchen through which they had all looked so many times but never together like this, and they looked for some evidence of the event they feared most, and they looked in every direction but could not see the past because time doesn't move in that direction, and so they looked for a long while and nobody saw anything at all.

Honey

Antonio Ungar

M Y SISTER IS alone on this side of the post fence, standing on the red earth, under the noonday light. I am looking at her from next to the columns on the patio. She has done something forbidden and without hesitating for a second she has walked right up to the fence in order to show everybody (me, the silence of the garden) her limitless strength and seriousness. My sister is four years old. I'm six. She has smeared herself with the honey mama left in the kitchen: her arms, her legs under her short dress, and two blobs of honey on her cheeks. And now, alone, in the middle of the garden, under that totalizing light, deformed by the heat that rises from the earth between us, separating us, she defies the world, she smiles and waits. Little by little her body begins to transform, getting thicker and darker.

Thousands of bees from the neighbors' gardens, from the honeycombs at the tops of the silk cotton trees, from the guava trees, head for my sister's body that stands as still as a totem pole, defying the sun and the clouds of smoke, defying the entire tropics with her stillness and her serious little-girl smile. I feel like I'm going to choke from fear and the good fortune of being able to participate in this ritual, that I'm going to faint out of admiration for that girl who is no longer a girl but rather a stiff body thousands of bees are walking on without stinging her (not one attacks her, as if they know how powerful she is), bees who are enjoying the honey, piled on top of each other, a swarm of restless little living beings, crazed, who deform my sister and make her magical, awesome, standing and still in the middle of the garden.

A while later, as if in a dream, in a painting cut up into pure colors, into absolute oil colors, comes the image of mama with her hands raised high above her head, dressed in a long green dress, mama running through the garden and shouting, her body trembling (I watch her, without moving), pulling my sister by the hand and feeling the first stings, the first of many stings that will leave her in a rocking chair for a week, swollen and sad. Holding my sister by one hand and waving the other arm, in pain, crazed, mama runs to the pool on the shady side of the house, picking up my sister who is immune to the bees who don't want to sting her, throws her in the water, all the way, she can stand in the pool with her head out of the water and from that head that's sticking out, my blond, freckle-faced sister, my beautiful sister with cat eyes, surrounded by bees buzzing around her and drowning, with perfect white teeth, with pink lips, is laughing. Gales of laughter. She doesn't stop laughing and she keeps laughing when mama, defeated, sits on the edge of the cement deck of the pool, places her head in her hands, looks at the red earth between her feet, and cries. For her pain, for her rage, for that daughter with green eyes who doesn't stop laughing.

Translated by Katherine Silver

Hotel Room

Juan José Saer

THE GUEST STARES at himself for a while in the mirror, deeply absorbed. His life and immediate tasks aren't enough to distract from his face, his naked body. He's gotten heavy, it seems. He's closing in on forty. Haven't women begun to not notice him now? A few years more and he'll be plainly elderly, one of these interchangeable old men wandering city streets, ignored by the crowd, anonymous and gray. In his youth he imagined old age to be the age of wisdom; lately it seems little more than a slow, inevitable reduction to animal. For years lived, all that remains is fallible flesh.

But these thoughts pass quickly. His traveling companion, having lingered at the beach, bursts abruptly into the bathroom and, brushing past, begins undressing beside the tub. The man contemplates her in the mirror: the girl's firm suntanned body is even more striking and wild as she unties her hair—with two or three skillful flips it spills onto her shoulders. Later, she scrubs her body vigorously under the spigot, eyes closed, head raised as if by instinct to deflect heavy rain. The memory of his own fallibility dissolves, swept away by this dense, persistent presence, this vivid living lump occupying the brilliant bathroom granting it substance and meaning.

While he pays the bill in the restaurant, the girl decides that this man she's lived with fifteen months hasn't surrendered his secrets. Why the silence, these somber looks, the abrupt answers followed by (one can't help but observe) immediate, heartfelt apologies? On the outside, yes, he would appear to be healthy, he's very sturdy and lively. The man's unease, the girl tells herself now, wouldn't seem bad if it were hers: I'm fairly unstable, she thinks, and my demands for constancy, for unstinting support, are for him perhaps an unbearable burden. I'll be more open from now on, she thinks generously, to fleeting living, and not try so hard to arrange things beforehand. As they leave the restaurant, the girl—having defeated (with optimism, or perhaps resignation) her difficult thoughts—abandons herself to the man's gracious gesture, his arm on her shoulders drawing her close to his chest. Slowly and happily they cross the deserted city toward the hotel, where, slightly later, flung naked on the bed, post-copulation, they surrender themselves separately to their own thoughts, and that slow disintegration preceding sleep, which one might call the result of exhaustion, suspect as one may that the blackness it ends in is the true, ongoing state of mind, after all.

The hotel manager, working the counter all morning, sees them exit the elevator a little before noon. He hands them the bill and takes their money, retaining the change— the guest, tipping his head toward the upper floors, indicates it should be left for the maids. After the pair disappear past the spacious half-open door, he forgets them at once, secreting the original bill (the duplicate went with the guest) between the leaves of a hidden ledger he carries; such double accounting helps soften his taxes. At this hour in the lobby—a bit pretentious, passé—no one is here. The September sun streams in the wide window facing the boulevard. The armchairs are empty, the TV is off. For two or three minutes nothing happens at all (the man immobile beside the counter, thinking his thoughts). Then there's the familiar thud of the elevator, summoned from above, echoing in the brightly lit lobby.

Translated by Kirk Nesset

The Nihilist

Ron Carlson

H E WAS ON a plane again and now it was late, he'd missed a connection in Denver, and the west was dark and the big plane flew west in the night. It was half full and the people had spread out and the men were sprawled on three seats sleeping where they could. The steward had come by and brought him a coffee where he worked alone in a row at the back of the plane and then she brought him three packages of cookies and smiled and said, Knock yourself out. He looked at her and said, I'm not even on this plane. I was on the earlier one. He was tired now for the first time on his long trip, five or six cities, and the hotels and he had held up and then today the fall sun had laid itself across the hills of Utah in a way he recognized and loved and it hurt him, such beauty, and it seemed to be change itself and change had been a hard teacher for the man for these years, and he was sick of beauty and he was sick of change, but it didn't stop them from cracking his heart. My fucking heart's cracked, he had said to himself so long ago now. And now, on the plane, he was just tired. Your heart, he said aloud. Who cares. Who fucking cares. It helped and felt good to use profanity when he was tired. It was lovely to spit ugly questions full of profanity when you were tired. The plane was roaring its whisper and he didn't even care now. He had wanted to get home for some reason and now he would get there and who cared. He was smiling with his new nihilism. He was quite the fucking nihilist. Oh, he could zero with the best of them. He could out-nothing the heavyweights. Then his nihilism grew thin and he was simply alone on a plane far from earth. His nihilism was fraudulent. He twisted his mouth in a way he sometimes did when vexed and now he was vexed as a fraudulent nihilist. He cared about too much. He could marshal his fucking nihilism for about five seconds and then the world came up for him, all the people he cared for came up for him, their names, and he was kept by the names and the faces of these people from going again to the litany of nothings. He wanted care in his life. He exhibited care. He was capable of it. Fucking care. He was smiling again, so tired. It has been a long day and he'd been careful in it. Something good had happened, he knew, more than one thing really, and he had it in his pocket. The steward came by with her big silver bracelet and brought him more coffee much too late on a Friday night for coffee, but of course. He's typing on a plane, drinking coffee and the woman was somewhere safe and sound. That was all he needed to know. Oh, my heck, the woman. He was now thinking of the woman in her pajamas in her yellow sheets sleeping and now his smile was the real smile, the one that fit his face like a sunset. He was on a plane again, and though it felt so fucking much like the end of something in his fatigue, he knew with true gravity that everything would be all right.

POLAND

Stories

Natasza Goerke

STORY #1, "BREAKUP": I broke up.
Story #2, "Memory": I remembered.
Story #3, "The Comeback": I came back.
And so on.

The stories are short, but concise. No need to scrutinize
them. The final sentence is contained in the first. Saves all
sorts of time. Who cares about the rest. All that paper in
between. There's one for everyone. Narratives, inventories,
notes. Read it ages ago.

And the fact that I was breaking up? That I remembered?
That I was on my way back? Who hasn't heard it all before!
A label is enough: an abbreviation, a title, any old crap, and
all at once it all comes back.

Remembers. Breaks up.

Whoever doesn't get this, he'll never figure it out. No
matter how he scrutinizes it. All those sheets of paper in
between. He won't figure out what it means. To break up,
to remember, to come back. And so on.

Translated by W. Martin

FLASH
THEORY

O the great God of Theory, he's just a pencil stub, a chewed stub with a worn eraser at the end of a huge scribble.

Charles Simic

I usually compare the novel to a mammal, be it wild as a tiger or tame as a cow; the short story to a bird or a fish; the microstory to an insect (iridescent in the best cases).

Luisa Valenzuela

I think of flash fiction, or the short short, as being more like a painting than like long fiction. The ambition of a short short is not to make readers "lose themselves"—how far lost can you get in a couple of pages?

Deb Olin Unferth

I am, on the whole, a person of few words. I studied in a convent in Karachi where the nuns said, "Economy in everything, including words."

Talat Abbasi

Why these things, now? Well, who is notable for making plans anymore? Who feels like the hero of an epic? These are tunes for the end of time, for those in an information age who are sick of data.

Charles Baxter

Writers who do short shorts need to be especially bold. They stake everything on a stroke of inventiveness.

Irving Howe

"Parting"

"Quick—a story! The bus is leaving!" she said. And so it was: the air brakes released like my will to stand gone faint. But I trotted along beside the open slash of window, into the wet street. I worked at the idea for a story as I ran faster. It would have to be good, and it would have to matter. I was on the verge of something when the bus got its second wind, suddenly, and I knew that the chorus of its pistons would rise above me. All I could do was position myself in the middle of the street, in newly-aged September light—hoping to be framed squarely by the black window of the bus. A small figure, with story.

Daryl Scroggins

Good one-page fictions have a spiral construction: the words circle out from a dense, packed core, and the spiral moves through the words, past the boundary of the page. That limitless quality could be said to apply to great fiction of any length, but the realized one-page fiction must move palpably beyond the page, like a ghost self . . . The one-page fiction should hang in the air of the mind like an image made of smoke.

Jayne Anne Phillips

THE APPEAL OF FLASH

What I love about exceptionally brief stories is the way that they often bring me to a point of recognition in a paragraph or two, and then leave me there, absolutely suspended. There is no gentle letdown, no winding down, no expulsion of air—just that wonderful moment.

Dinty W. Moore

Why are miniature things so compelling? . . .
The miniature is mysterious . . . .
Miniatures encourage attention . . . .
Miniatures are intimate . . . .
Time, in miniature form, like a gas compressed,
gets hotter.

Lia Purpura

The flame of complete combustion has a blue tinge. It is a beautiful color; it is a ferocious color. A piece of writing is powerful if its words are "completely combusted."

Chen Yizhi

Brevity is the face of mortality. No one blathers at the edge of the grave, except clergymen (and some writers), whose minds are on immortality, which gives them more time because it's presumed to go on forever—just as they often seem to.

Alvin Greenberg

⌒

Don't let it end like this. Tell them I said something.

Last Words of Pancho Villa

THE ESSENTIALS OF FLASH

It is condensed, even curt; its rhythms are fleeting, its languor quick, its majesty diminutive. It discredits accretions, honors reduction, and refuses to ramble. Its identity is exceptional, its appetite exclusive. It is refractory, rapid, runtish. It reverses, refutes, revises. It can do in a page what a novel does in two hundred. It covers years in less time, time in almost no time. It wants to deliver us where we were before we began. Its aim is restorative, to keep us young. It thrives on self-effacement, and generates statements, on its own behalf, that are shorn or short. Its end is erasure.

Mark Strand

⌒

"God is in the details." Flaubert's aphorism is often recalled when speaking about microhistory, the intensive historical investigation of a small area . . . .

Similarly to classical Greek plays, where we can find a threefold unity of place, time and action, the microhistorical approach creates a focal point, and in this focus the subject of the historical investigation can be studied with an intensity unparalleled in studies about nations, states or social groupings, stretching over decades, centuries or whatever *longue durée*.

István Szijártó

⌐

Very short fictions are nearly always experimental, exquisitely calibrated, reminiscent of Frost's definition of a poem—a structure of words that consumes itself as it unfolds, like ice melting on a stove . . . .

There are those for whom one of Chopin's brilliant little Preludes is worth an entire symphony by one or another "classic" composer whose method is to build upon repetition and contrast.

Joyce Carol Oates

⌐

It's its own self, and it's intrinsically different from the short story and more like the sonnet or ghazal—two quick moves in opposite directions, dialectical moves, perhaps, and then a leap to a radical resolution that leaves the reader anxious in a particularly satisfying way. The source, the need, for the form seems to me to be the same need that created Norse kennings, Zen koans, Sufi tales, where language and metaphysics grapple for holds like Greek wrestlers, and not the need that created the novel or the short story, even, where language and the social sciences sleep peacefully inside one another like bourgeois spoons.

Russell Banks

⌐

For me, a very short story should do four basic things: obviously it should tell a story; it should be entertaining; it should be thought-provoking; and, if done well enough, it should invoke an emotional response.

Robert Swartwood

FLASH FICTION OR PROSE POETRY?

I never understood the debate about flash fiction: Is it a story; is it a poem? It isn't a poem because the author doesn't *want* it to be a poem. When a poet writes a prose poem and says, "This is a prose poem," everyone says okay and that's that. But when a flash fiction writer says, "This is a story," there's often a collective stomping of brakes on the writing highway as naysayers screech to a halt to gauge its storyness. Don't be afraid, I want to tell those naysayers. It's just a little story. Like a long story, but shorter.

Sherrie Flick

The truth is people are kind of scared by very very short stories—just as they are by long poems.

A short story is closer to the poem than to the novel (I've said that a million times) and when it's very very short—1, 2, 2½ pages—should be read like a poem. That is slowly. People who like to skip can't skip in a 3-page story.

Grace Paley

For me, the difference between a flash fiction and a prose poem of similar length is in its treatment of time via the sentence. A flash fiction, however dense and lyrical, operates (like any fiction) through cause-effect, action and consequence, and so even when it engages memory it treats time as moving forward with the sentence. The prose poem, like the lyric poem, is recursive in nature, not because of but despite the fact that the sentence is its central unit. Lacking the line, which inherently retards time, it finds other ways to frustrate the momentum of the sentence, and through that frustration it opens into the swiftly dilating but not forward-moving lyric moment.

Katharine Coles

On the Time Difference Between Poetry and Prose

The wall clock read one minute after midnight. A poet and a writer met. "My muse," said the writer, "has deserted me." The poet responded, "So write about it." The writer wept softly. "And she is with someone else right now." The poet said, "So write about it." The writer said, "But I suspect that he has blue eyes." "So write about it," the poet advised, "or just beat him up." "Maybe she didn't love me," said the writer. "Yes, maybe she never loved me." The poet said, "So write about it. Or beat him up. Is he strong?" "I didn't say that he was strong," objected the writer, "I said that he had blue eyes." "So write about it." "Tell me, what is it that you want from me?" shouted the writer, "*you* write about it." The poet said with surprise, "Why suggest that I write?" "Because you suggested it to me," answered the writer. "You advised me to write." "I didn't advise you to do anything," said the poet, shrugging. "What do you mean—you suggested it. Five times." "I don't know what you're talking about." "About my muse leaving me . . ." "So write about it . . ." "You see, again you . . ." The writer jumped up, tore the clock from the wall

and struck the poet with all his might. The time was three
minutes after midnight.

Alex Epstein

THE LONG AND SHORT OF IT

If a writer of prose knows enough of what he is writing
about he may omit things that he knows and the reader,
if the writer is writing truly enough, will have a feeling
of those things as strongly as though the writer had stated
them. The dignity of movement of an iceberg is due to
only one-eighth of it being above water. A writer who
omits things because he does not know them only makes
hollow places in his writing.

Ernest Hemingway

It is laborious and impoverishing madness to compose
vast books, to expound over five hundred pages an idea
that orally can be expressed perfectly well in a few
minutes.

Jorge Luis Borges

Stories can be as short as a sentence.

Randall Jarrell

It is my ambition to say in ten sentences what others say in
a whole book.

Friedrich Nietzsche

I have the feeling that [my] little stories are a bit like novels from which all the air has been removed. And that might be my definition of a novel: forty lines plus two cubic meters of air. I've settled for simply the forty lines: they take up less space. And with books, of course, you know that space is always an enormous problem.

Giorgio Manganelli

When a story is compressed so much, the matter of it tends to require more size: that is, in order to make it work in so small a space its true subject must be proportionately larger.

Richard Bausch

When I start to write a very short story, I always imagine it as a novel. In some parallel universe, there must be a crazy writer who is actually writing those novels.

Alex Epstein

A good short-short is short but not small, light but not slight.

Ku Ling

Brevity is the soul of wit.

William Shakespeare

Brevity is the sister of talent.

Anton Chekhov

❧

Flash fiction is re-incarnated brevity. In our warming world, brevity is green. In our world of competing media, brevity is nimble. In our world where time is the most precious commodity, brevity is eternal.

Mark Budman

❧

The Soul's distinct connection
With immortality
Is best disclosed by Danger
Or quick Calamity—

As Lightning on a Landscape
Exhibits Sheets of Place—
Not yet suspected—but for Flash—
And Click—and Suddenness.

Emily Dickinson

THE ART OF FLASH

Kill your darlings, kill your darlings, even when it breaks your egocentric little scribbler's heart, kill your darlings.

Stephen King

❧

The difference between the right word and the almost

right word is the difference between lightning and the lightning bug.

Mark Twain

A short short is not a single thing done a single way. So many are sharp, luminescent puzzles, arresting flashes in the dark that leave us a touch of wonder or alarm. Some are complete little worlds in a page and some are simply scene fragments in two. Of course at times there is word-play and often slanted imagery, even the jarring moment. Often the jarring moment. Some are tricky seductions, some brash and confrontational. Many start and then stop and either you feel like you missed a step or you get the joke. The language can prance, which is a kind of walk that takes you in a circle.

Ron Carlson

The letter I have written today is longer than usual because I lacked the time to make it shorter.

Blaise Pascal

Every sentence, every phrase, every word has to fight for its life.

Crawford Kilian

Get in, get out. Don't linger. Go on.

Raymond Carver

Omit needless words.

William Strunk

I try to leave out the parts that people skip.

Elmore Leonard

THE CULTURE OF FLASH

The first story ever, I read somewhere, appears on an ancient Egyptian tablet and declares that "John went out on a trip." How do we know this is a flash fiction and not a document? Because no one during that time period could have left his town on his own will. Moreover, it encapsulates the high rhetoric of sudden fiction: it has a character (I call him "John," but he has 1,000 names); there is a dominant action (the story-telling is fully present); and what is shown or said happens in time. Not less important, it announces the very rule of any story—the breaking of a code. John is an adventurer who stands against authority and decides to leave, to explore, to know.

Julio Ortega

Microfiction is the writing of the new millennium, for it is very close to the paratactic fragmentation of the hypertextual writing of the electronic age.

Lauro Zavala

⟍⟋

A contributing factor to the genre's future dissemination is that short-shorts are both device-independent and compatible with today's technology. They offer relative freedom from censorship not enjoyed in other media.

Aili Mu and Julie Chiu

⟍⟋

Flash Fiction, or *wei xing xiao shuo*, as it is known in China today, also goes by the name of Minute Story, Pocket-Size Story, Palm-Size Story, and, perhaps most evocatively and, in my opinion, most accurately (for China at least)—Smoke-Long Story, which promises to let the reader relish the sights and sounds of an entire make-believe world before he or she has time to finish one delicious cigarette.

Shouhua Qi

⟍⟋

The king died and then the queen died is a story. The king died, and then the queen died of grief is a plot.

E. M. Forster

Grief

The King died. Long live the King. And then the Queen died. She was buried beside him. The King died and then the Queen died of grief. This was the posted report. And no one said a thing. But you can't die of grief. It can take away your appetite and keep you in your chamber, but not forever. It isn't terminal. Eventually you'll come out and want a toddy. The Queen died subsequent to the King, but not of grief. I know the royal coroner, have seen him around, a young guy with a good job. The death rate for the royalty is so much lower than that of the general populace. The coroner was summoned by the musicians, found her on the bedroom floor, checked for a pulse, and wrote "Grief" on the form. It looked good. And it was necessary. It answered the thousand questions about the state of the nation.

He didn't examine the body, perform an autopsy. If he had, he wouldn't have found grief. "There is no place for grief in the body." He would have found a blood alcohol level of one point nine and he would have found a clot of improperly chewed tangerine in the lady's throat which she had ingested while laughing.

But this seems a fine point. The Queen is dead. Long live her grief. Long live the Duke of Reddington and the Earl of Halstar who were with me that night entertaining the Queen in her chambers. She was a vigorous sort. And long live the posted report which will always fill a royal place in this old kingdom.

Ron Carlson

FLASH THEORY SOURCES

Abbasi, Talat, from her author commentary in the "Afternotes" section of *Sudden Fiction International*.

Banks, Russell, from the "Afterwords" section of *Sudden Fiction: American Short-Short Stories*.

Bausch, Richard, from his interview in *Five Points* magazine.

Baxter, Charles, from the "Afterwords" section of *Sudden Fiction: American Short-Short Stories*.

Borges, Jorge Luis, from the prologue to his book *The Garden of Forking Paths*. Quotation translated by Daniel Tunnard.

Budman, Mark, from his essay "Expose Yourself to Flash," in *The Rose Metal Press Field Guide to Writing Flash Fiction*, edited by Tara L. Masih.

Carlson, Ron, "A short short is not a single thing done in a single way," from his introduction to Claudia Smith's *The Sky Is a Well and Other Shorts*.

Carlson, Ron, "Grief," from *Micro Fiction: An Anthology of Really Short Stories*, edited by Jerome Stern.

Carver, Raymond, from "A Storyteller's Shoptalk," an article in *The New York Times*, February 15, 1981, in the Books section.

Chekhov, Anton, from his letter to A. P. Chekhov, April 11, 1889.

Chen, Yizhi, from *Loud Sparrows: Contemporary Chinese Short-Shorts*, edited and translated by Aili Mu, Julie Chiu, and Howard Goldblatt.

Coles, Katharine. Original statement written for *Flash Fiction International*, first articulated at the Writers@Work Conference, Alta, Utah, June 2013.

Dickinson, Emily, Poem #974.

Epstein, Alex. "On the Time Difference Between Poetry and Prose" is from his book *Blue Has No South*. Translation by Becka Mara McKay.

Epstein, Alex, from the journal *World Literature Today*, September 2012, in the interview section of the feature "Very Short Fiction."

Flick, Sherrie, from her essay "Flash in a Pan: Writing Outside of Time's Boundaries," in *The Rose Metal Press Field Guide to Writing Flash Fiction*, edited by Tara L. Masih.

Forster, E. M., from *Aspects of the Novel*.

Greenberg, Alvin, from "Why Is the Short Story Short and the Short-Short Even Shorter?," in the "Afterwords" section of *Sudden Fiction: American Short-Short Stories*.

Hemingway, Ernest, from *Death in the Afternoon*.

Howe, Irving, from his introduction to *Short Shorts: An Anthology of Shortest Stories*, edited by Irving Howe and Ilana Wiener Howe.

Jarrell, Randall, from his introduction, "Stories," to *The Anchor Book of Stories*.

Kilian, Crawford, from his book *Writing for the Web*.

King, Stephen, from his book *On Writing: A Memoir of the Craft*.

Ku Ling, from *Loud Sparrows: Contemporary Chinese Short-Shorts*, edited and translated by Aili Mu, Julie Chiu, and Howard Goldblatt.

Leonard, Elmore, from the *New York Times* series Writers on

Writing: "Easy on the Adverbs, Exclamation Points and Especially Hooptedoodle," by Elmore Leonard, July 16, 2001.

Manganelli, Giorgio, quoted on the dust jacket of his book *Centuria: One Hundred Ouroboric Novels*, 2005.

Moore, Dinty W., from "The Moment of Truth: An Introduction," in *Sudden Stories: The MAMMOTH Book of Miniscule Fiction*, edited by Dinty W. Moore.

Mu, Aili, and Julie Chiu. *Loud Sparrows: Contemporary Chinese Short-Shorts*, edited and translated by Aili Mu, Julie Chiu, and Howard Goldblatt.

Nietzsche, Friedrich, from *Twilight of the Idols*.

Oates, Joyce Carol, from the "Afternotes" section of *Sudden Fiction International*.

Ortega, Julio, from his essay "A Flash before the Bang," in *The Rose Metal Press Field Guide to Writing Flash Fiction*, edited by Tara L. Masih.

Paley, Grace, from the "Afterwords" section of *Sudden Fiction: American Short-Short Stories*.

Pascal, Blaise, from a collection of letters called "Lettres provinciales," 1657. First English translation 1658, *Les Provinciales, or, The Mystery of Jesuitisme* by Blaise Pascal, Letter 16: Postscript, printed for Richard Royston, London.

Phillips, Jayne Anne, from her essay "'Cheers,' (or) How I Taught Myself to Write," in *The Rose Metal Press Field Guide to Writing Flash Fiction*, edited by Tara L. Masih.

Purpura, Lia, adapted with her permission from section lead-ins in her essay "On Miniatures" in the journal *Brevity* (in the Craft Essays section).

Qi, Shouhua, from his essay "Old Wine in New Bottles?: Flash Fiction from Contemporary China," in *The Rose Metal Field Guide to Writing Flash Fiction*, edited by Tara L. Masih.

Scroggins, Daryl. "Parting" is from his collection *This Is Not the Way We Came In*.

Shakespeare, William, from *Hamlet*, spoken by Polonius in Act 2, Scene 2.

Simic, Charles, from his book *The World Doesn't End*.

Strand, Mark, from the "Afterwords" section of *Sudden Fiction: American Short-Short Stories*.

Strunk, William, from *The Elements of Style*, by William Strunk Jr. and E. B. White.

Swartwood, Robert, from his introduction to *Hint Fiction: An Anthology of Stories in 25 Words or Fewer*, edited by Robert Swartwood.

Szijártó, István, from "Four Arguments for Microhistory" in *Rethinking History* 6:2, in the section "Miniatures."

Unferth, Deb Olin, from her essay "Put Yourself in Danger: An Examination of Diane Williams's Courageous Short," in *The Rose Metal Press Field Guide to Writing Flash Fiction*, edited by Tara L. Masih.

Valenzuela, Luisa, from her introduction to *Sudden Fiction Latino*.

Villa, Pancho, in Andrea Saenz's story "Everyone's *Abuelo* Can't Have Ridden with Pancho Villa," in *Sudden Fiction Latino*. She notes that Nicholas Casey reported in his online article in *The Wall Street Journal*, April 15, 2010, "According to the lore, his final words were: 'It shouldn't end this way. Tell them I said something.'"

Zavala, Lauro, from his first article on the subject, delivered at the first international conference on minifiction, 1998, held in Mexico City. Translation by Steven J. Stewart. The full article is in the first issue of the e-journal *El Cuento en Red*.

CONTRIBUTOR NOTES

Daniel Alarcón was born in Lima, Peru, and grew up in Birmingham, Alabama. In 2010, *The New Yorker* named him one of the best 20 Writers Under 40, and his most recent novel, *At Night We Walk in Circles*, was a finalist for the 2013 PEN/Faulkner Award. He is executive producer of *Radio Ambulante*, a Spanish-language narrative journalism podcast.

Sherman Alexie grew up on the Spokane Indian Reservation. Among his best-known works are the story collection *The Lone Ranger and Tonto Fistfight in Heaven*, and the film *Smoke Signals*, based on a story from that collection for which he cowrote the screenplay. A few of his most recent awards are the National Book Award for Young People's Literature, the Odyssey Award for best audiobook for young people (read by Alexie), and the PEN/Faulkner Award for Fiction. He lives in Seattle, Washington.

Chris Andrews is an Australian writer, translator, and teacher whose translations include books by Roberto Bolaño and César Aira. He is the author of a critical study, *Poetry and Cosmogony:*

Science in the Writing of Queneau and Ponge, and a collection of poems, *Cut Lunch*.

Edgar Omar Avilés was born in 1980 in Morelia, Michoacán. He is the author of several books, including *La noche es luz de un sol negro*, *Guiichi*, *Luna Cinema*, *Cabalgata en duermevela*, and *No respiramos: inflamos fantasmas*. His stories have appeared in *The Best Mexican Short Stories*.

Juan José Barrientos is the author of *Versiones*, *Ficción-historia*, and *La gata revolcada*. He is especially concerned with the rewriting or recycling of literary works. He studied at the University of Heidelberg, was a lecturer at the Sorbonne, and has taught at the University of Veracruz for many years.

Jensen Beach, author of the story collection *For Out of the Heart Proceed*, teaches at the University of Illinois. His stories and reviews have appeared widely in literary magazines and he is a web editor at *Hobart*.

Ari Mikael Behn is a Norwegian author and husband of Princess Märtha Louise. He has published three novels and two collections of short stories.

Georgia Birnie has had a lifelong interest in languages and has lived in Central America and France. She lives in Auckland, New Zealand, where she is completing a master's degree in psychology.

Roberto Bolaño was a Chilean author of novels, short stories, poems, and essays. In 1999, he won the Rómulo Gallegos Prize for his novel *Los detectives salvajes* (*The Savage Detectives*), and in 2008 he was posthumously awarded the National Book Critics Circle Award for Fiction for his novel *2666*. He has been described by *The New York Times* as "the most significant Latin American literary voice of his generation."

Elena Bossi is an Argentine poet, essayist, literary critic, and editor whose work has been published in numerous magazines and journals. Her many books include *Rags* and *Magical Beings of Argentina*.

Juan Carlos Botero is a Colombian writer and journalist. Winner of the Juan Rulfo Short Story Award, he has published two novels, two books of essays, and two collections of short stories. One collection, *The Seeds of Time: Epiphanies*, has been heralded as "a new genre of literature."

Nathan Budoff is an artist who has exhibited in Boston, New York, Chicago, Bogotá, Medellín, San Juan, Santa Fe, and Minnesota. He is an associate professor of art at the University of Puerto Rico and continues to exhibit regularly with Galería 356 in San Juan.

Ron Carlson is the author of ten books of fiction, including the novel *The Signal*. His newest novel is *Return to Oakpine*. His short stories have appeared in *Esquire, Harper's, The Atlantic*, and other journals and anthologies. He is the director of the graduate program in fiction at the University of California, Irvine.

Antoine Cassar has translated a number of his fellow Maltese authors into English; he is also an avid translator into Maltese of Neruda, Whitman, and Tagore. His poem *Merħba* won the United Planet Writing Prize in 2009; his poem *Passport* has been published in eight languages.

José Chaves holds an MFA in creative writing from the University of Oregon. In 1999 he published a bilingual anthology of Latin American sudden fiction titled *The Book of Brevity*; selections from it were reprinted in the anthology *Sudden Fiction Latino*. His most recent book, *The Contract of Love*, is a memoir about his quixotic Colombian father.

Chen Qiyou was born in 1953. He is a professor of Chinese at a teachers' college in Taiwan.

Alberto Chimal is one of Mexico's most prolific writers of experimental fiction, including flash and Twitter fiction. In the United States his work has appeared in *World Literature Today* and *The Kenyon Review*. He is author of the novels *Los esclavos* and *La torre y el jardín* as well as many books of short fiction.

Nuala Ní Chonchúir lives in Galway, Ireland. Her fourth short story collection, *Mother America*, was published in 2012, a chapbook of short-short stories in 2013 in the United States, and her second novel in 2014.

James Claffey was born and raised in Dublin, Ireland. His work has appeared in many magazines; he is the author of a book of stories, *Blood a Cold Blue*, and the editor of a story collection, *Daddy Cool*.

Margaret Jull Costa has been a literary translator for nearly thirty years and has translated novels and short stories by such writers as Eça de Queiroz, Fernando Pessoa, José Saramago, Javier Marías, and Bernardo Atxaga. Her most recent award was the 2012 Calouste Gulbenkian Translation Prize for Teolinda Gersão's *The Word Tree*.

Jim Crace has published novels, short stories, and radio plays. He has won many awards, including the National Book Critics Circle Award, and has been shortlisted three times for the Booker Prize. He lives in Birmingham, England, with his wife and two children.

Marco Denevi was an Argentine writer well known for very short stories. His first novel was a bestseller in several languages and adapted for film. His story "Secret Ceremony" was made into a film starring Elizabeth Taylor. He died in 1998.

Natalie Diaz, a member of the Mojave and Pima Indian tribes, attended Old Dominion University on a full athletic scholarship. After playing professional basketball in Austria, Portugal, Spain, Sweden, and Turkey, she returned to Old Dominion for an MFA in writing. She was selected for Best New Poets and won the Nimrod/Hardman Pablo Neruda Prize for Poetry. She lives in Surprise, Arizona.

Linh Dinh is the author of five books of poetry and three of prose, including a novel, *Love Like Hate*. *The Village Voice* picked Dinh's *Blood and Soap*, which has the most generous sampling of his flash fictions, as one of the best books of 2004.

Brian Doyle is the editor of *Portland* magazine at the University of Portland and the author of many books of essays, "proems," and fiction, notably the sprawling novels *Mink River* and *The Plover*.

Patricia Dubrava is a poet, essayist, and translator whose recent translations have appeared in the journals *Reunion: The Dallas Review*, *Metamorphoses*, and *The Cafe Irreal*, and the anthology *New-Border: Contemporary Voices from the Texas/Mexico Border*. Dubrava lives in Denver.

Lane Dunlop was a critically acclaimed translator of French poetry and pre-1960s Japanese literature. His translation of *The Late Chrysanthemum: Twenty-one Stories from the Japanese* won the Japan–United States Friendship Award for Literary Translation, and the American Academy of Arts and Letters recognized him with an Academy Award in Literature. He died in 2013.

Stuart Dybek is especially known for his very short stories; flash fiction figures prominently in several of his books, especially his most recent collection, *Ecstatic Cahoots*. His awards include a MacArthur Fellowship, a PEN/Malamud Prize, a Rea Award for the Short Story, and a Lannan Award for Innovation in the Short Story.

Berit Ellingsen is a Korean-Norwegian author whose stories have appeared in anthologies and literary journals, including *Unstuck*, *Bluestem*, *SmokeLong Quarterly*, *Metazen*, and *decomP magazinE*. Her collection of short stories is *Beneath the Skin*. Berit admits, when abroad, to pining for the fjords.

Nathan Englander, co-translator of Etgar Keret's *Suddenly A Knock at the Door*, is author of the story collections *What We Talk About When We Talk About Anne Frank* and *For the Relief of Unbearable Urges*, as well as the novel *The Ministry of Special Cases*. He has won the Frank O'Connor International Short Story Award and was a finalist for the 2013 Pulitzer Prize.

Tony Eprile is a South African writer who has long been living in the United States. His novel *The Persistence of Memory* was a *New York Times* Notable Book. He has taught at universities abroad and in the United States, including the Iowa Writers' Workshop. His story "The Interpreter for the Tribunal" stems from something Desmond Tutu said: that simultaneous interpreters at the Truth and Reconciliation hearings, who had to speak in the first person for both the victims of violence and the perpetrators of it, often had nervous breakdowns.

Alex Epstein (see his story in Flash Theory) was born in Leningrad (now St. Petersburg) and moved to Israel when he was eight years old. His four collections of short stories and three novels have been translated into eight languages. His collections of short-short stories, *Blue Has No South* and *Lunar Savings Time*, are available in English.

Josefina Estrada is a Mexican story writer, novelist, and journalist. Among her books are the story collection *Malagato* and the novels *Desde que Díos amance* and *Virgen de medianoche*. Her work has previously appeared in English in *Storm: New Writing from Mexico* and *Sudden Fiction Latino: Short-Short Stories from the United States and Latin America*.

Muna Fadhil is an Iraqi humanitarian worker and advocate whose main passion is refugees, women's rights, and ethnic and religious tolerance. Muna mainly writes about her experiences living in wars, under economic sanctions, and with ongoing violence, determined to shed light on these issues.

Robert Ferguson was born in the UK, where he studied Norwegian in the Scandinavian Studies course at University College, London. He immigrated in 1983 to Norway. He is the award-winning author of radio plays for the BBC, literary biographies, a history of the Vikings, and two novels.

Anne O. Fisher made her career debut with the critically acclaimed renditions of Ilya Ilf and Evgeny Petrov's novels *The Twelve Chairs* and *The Little Golden Calf*. She has also translated the prose of Polina Klyukina, Ksenia Buksha, Leonid Tishkov, Marina Moskvina, and Margarita Meklina, and, with cotranslator Derek Mong, the poetry of Maxim Amelin.

Ezra E. Fitz began his literary life at Princeton University, studying under the tutelage of James Irby, C. K. Williams, Jonathan Galassi, and Robert Fagles. His translations of contemporary Latin American literature by Alberto Fuguet and Eloy Urroz have been praised by *The New Yorker*, *The Washington Post*, and *The Believer*, among other publications. He lives with his wife in Tennessee.

Rubem Fonseca is for many critics Brazil's greatest living author. His novels and short stories have appeared in a dozen languages, and he has received numerous literary awards, including the Camões Prize, considered the Nobel of Portuguese-language literature.

Marcela Fuentes is a south Texan living in Atlanta with her husband and small son. A graduate of the Iowa Writers' Workshop, she has published fiction in *Indiana Review*, *Vestal Review*, *Blackbird*, and other journals, and her stories are anthologized in *Best of the Web* and *New Stories from the Southwest*.

Alberto Fuguet is a Chilean writer of short stories and novels who is also a film critic and director. In 1999 *Time* named him one of the fifty most important Latin American writers of the new millennium.

Avital Gad-Cykman is an Israeli writer living in Brazil. Her short stories, including flash fiction, have appeared in anthologies and in journals such as *McSweeney's*, *Glimmer Train*, *Prism International*, *Michigan Quarterly Review*, and *Stand* (UK). Her collection of flash fiction is *Life In, Life Out*.

Petina Gappah is a Zimbabwean writer with law degrees from Cambridge, the University of Graz, and the University of Zimbabwe. She is author of *An Elegy for Easterly: Stories*; her short fiction and essays have been published in eight countries. She lives with her son Kush in Geneva, where she works as counsel in an international organization.

Natazsa Goerke was born in Poznań, Poland. Her four books have been published in Polish as well as in German, Slovak, and Croatian; her stories have appeared in numerous magazines and anthologies. In the mid-eighties she emigrated from Poland and after living for a time in Asia now lives in Hamburg.

Edith Grossman is well known for her translations of major Latin American authors such as Carlos Fuentes, Gabriel García Márquez, and Mario Vargas Llosa. She was awarded the PEN Ralph Manheim Medal in 2006 for her body of work, and, in 2010, the Queen Sofía Spanish Institute Translation Prize.

Judd Hampton lives in rural northern Alberta, Canada, with his wife, two children, two dogs, two cats, and two trucks. He works in the oilfield pushing natural gas toward your furnace. His stories have been nominated for the Journey Prize, National Magazine Award, Best American Short Stories, and, twice, the Pushcart Prize.

George Henson is the translator of two collections of short fiction, Elena Poniatowska's *The Heart of the Artichoke* and Luis Jorge Boone's *The Cannibal Night*. His translations have appeared in numerous journals, including *The Kenyon Review*, *The Literary Review*, *World Literature Today*, and *Words Without Borders*.

Tania Hershman was born in London, moved to Jerusalem in her twenties, and returned to England to serve as writer-in-residence in the Faculty of Science at Bristol University. A science journalist for thirteen years, she gave it up to write fiction and now has two story collections, both of which include flash fiction: *My Mother Was an Upright Piano* and *The White Road and Other Stories*. She is founder and editor of *The Short Review*.

Michael Hoffman has translated numerous books from the German, most recently *Joseph Roth: A Life in Letters* and *Impromptus: Selected Poems and Some Prose*, by Gottfried Benn. He is also a widely published, award-winning poet, editor, and critic. He is a professor in the Department of English at the University of Florida.

Randa Jarrar grew up in Kuwait and Egypt, and moved to the United States at the age of thirteen. She is the author of the novel *A Map of Home*, which won the Hopwood Prize and the Arab American Book Award. Her work has appeared in *The New York Times Magazine*, *Salon*, *Ploughshares*, *Utne Reader*, *Rumpus*, and others. She lives in Central California.

Ian Johnston was for many years a college and university teacher and is now an emeritus professor at the University of Vancouver Island. He is the author of *The Ironies of War: An Introduction to Homer's Iliad* and has translated several classic works from Greek, Latin, French, and German.

Franz Kafka, 1883–1924, wrote novels (*The Trial*), short stories ("The Metamorphosis," "A Hunger Artist"), and very short stories. He was one of the most influential writers of the twentieth century.

Toshiya Kamei holds an MFA in literary translation from the University of Arkansas. His translations include Liliana Blum's *The Curse of Eve and Other Stories*, Naoko Awa's *The Fox's Window and Other Stories*, Espido Freire's *Irlanda*, and Selfa Chew's *Silent Herons*.

Yasunari Kawabata was a Japanese short story writer and novelist whose works were influenced by Japanese Zen Buddhism and haiku and by European Dadaism and Expressionism. He won the Nobel Prize for Literature in 1968, becoming the first Japanese recipient of the award.

Etgar Keret is an Israeli writer known for his short stories, graphic novels, and scriptwriting for film and television. A number of his stories have been made into movies. His books have been translated into many languages.

Rashid Khattak was born and raised in the Karak district of Pakistan and took his master's degree in journalism from the University of Peshawar. He writes in Pashto, Urdu, and English, and translates from each to the others. He has worked with many media organizations.

Chi-young Kim is an award-winning literary translator based in Los Angeles. Her most recent works include Jung-myung Lee's

The Investigation, Sun-mi Hwang's *The Hen Who Dreamed She Could Fly*, and Kyung-sook Shin's *Please Look After Mom*, which won the Man Asian Literary Prize.

Kim Young-ha is a widely translated novelist, short story writer, screenwriter, and translator. His works have won Korea's top literary awards and been adapted for films and a musical.

Yin Ee Kiong is a Malaysian writer, social and political activist, and traveler. He has lived and worked in numerous countries, including Sudan and Papua New Guinea. He currently lives in Indonesia. His published works are *Postcards from a Foreign Country*, *Tin Man*, and *Out of the Tempurung*, of which he is coeditor.

Clifford E. Landers has translated some thirty book-length works from Portuguese, including novels by Rubem Fonseca, João Ubaldo Ribeiro, Jorge Amado, Patrícia Melo, Jô Soares, Chico Buarque, Ignácio de Loyola Brandão, Nélida Piñon, Paulo Coelho, Marcos Rey, and José de Alencar. He is a recipient of the Mário Ferreira Award and author of *Literary Translation: A Practical Guide*.

Tara Laskowski is the author of *Modern Manners for Your Inner Demons* and the senior editor of *SmokeLong Quarterly*. She lives in Virginia with her husband and son.

Mónica Lavín is a Mexican writer with eight collections of stories and eight novels. She won the Gilberto Owen Literary Prize for her short story collection *Ruby Tuesday no ha muerto*. Her 2009 novel *Yo, la peor* won the Elena Poniatowska Prize for Fiction. Her latest book of stories is *Manual para enamorarse*. Lavín lives in Mexico City.

Kirsty Logan lives in Glasgow, where she is the literary editor of *The List*. Her short fiction and poetry have been published in print and online and exhibited in galleries. Her debut collection of stories is *The Rental Heart and Other Fairytales*. Her first novel, *The Gracekeepers*, is forthcoming in 2015.

Robert Lopez is the author of two novels, *Part of the World* and *Kamby Bolongo Mean River*, and a story collection, *Asunder*. He has taught at the New School, Pratt Institute, Columbia University, and the Solstice MFA Creative Writing Program at Pine Manor College. He lives in Brooklyn, where he was born.

Antonio López Ortega is the Venezuelan author of six volumes of short stories. He studied literature in Caracas and Hispanic studies in Paris, and was a participant in the International Writing Program at the University of Iowa.

Naguib Mahfouz was an Egyptian novelist, short story writer, screenwriter, playwright, and columnist whose work during a seventy-year career has been translated into forty languages. In 1988 he received the Nobel Prize for Literature.

Luigi Malerba wrote short stories, historical novels, and screenplays. A leader of Italy's Neoavanguardia literary movement, he was the recipient of many prestigious awards. He died in 2008.

Giorgio Manganelli was an Italian journalist, translator, and fiction writer. Italo Calvino said that in Manganelli "Italian literature has . . . an inventor who is irresistible and inexhaustible in his games with language and ideas." Each "novel" in his collection *Centuria* is like an *ouroboros*, the ancient symbol of a serpent or dragon eating its own tail.

Alberto Manguel was born in Buenos Aires, lived in Israel when his father was ambassador there, then Italy, England, and Canada. He now lives in France, in a medieval presbytery renovated to house his thirty thousand books. Author of five novels, as well as an anthologist (*Black Water: The Book of Fantastic Literature*) and translator, he has received many prizes and two honorary doctorates.

Kuzhali Manickavel is the author of two short story collections, *Insects Are Just Like You and Me Except Some of Them Have Wings* and *Things We Found During the Autopsy.*

Henry Martin translates contemporary Italian literature and regularly contributes as a critic to a number of international art magazines. He lives with his wife and their son in the mountains of southern Tyrol not far from Bolzano, Italy.

W. Martin has published translations from German and Polish that include Michal Witkowski's *Lovetown*, Erich Kästner's *Emil and the Detectives*, and Natasza Goerke's *Farewells to Plasma*, as well as numerous works appearing in anthologies and journals. He has been a fiction editor at *Chicago Review* and in 2008 received the NEA Literature Fellowship for Translation.

W. Somerset Maugham, 1874–1965, was a widely traveled and popular British playwright, novelist, and story writer. Among his many novels are *Of Human Bondage* and *The Razor's Edge.* Some say his story "Appointment in Samarra" is based on a ninth-century Arabian Sufi story; others say the story's origins go back as far as the Babylonian Talmud.

Peter Zaragoza Mayshle, born and raised in the Philippines, received an MFA in creative writing from the University of Michigan, Ann Arbor and a Ph.D. from the University of Wisconsin, Madison. His stories have been published in his home country, the United States, Canada, and in *Flash: The International Short-Short Story Magazine* in England. He teaches at Hobart and William Smith Colleges.

Cate McGowan is a Georgia native whose short story collection *True Places Never Are* won the Moon City Press Inaugural Fiction Award. It will be published in 2015. Her stories have appeared in literary magazines and glossies such as *Glimmer Train*, *Snake Nation Review*, and *Tank*. She teaches at Valencia College in Florida.

Jon McGregor is a British novelist and highly awarded short story writer. His most recent book is the collection *This Isn't the Sort of Thing That Happens to Someone Like You*.

Anne McLean translates Latin American and Spanish novels, short stories, memoirs, and other writings by authors including Julio Cortázar, Héctor Abad, Evelio Rosero, Juan Gabriel Vásquez, Javier Cercas, Ignacio Martínez de Pisón, and Enrique Vila-Matas. She lives in Toronto.

Frankie McMillan is the author of *The Bag Lady's Picnic and Other Stories* and *Dressing for the Cannibals*. Her stories appear in *Best NZ Fiction* anthologies. In 2013 she was winner of the NZ National Flash Fiction Day award. She is a writer-in-residence at Canterbury University.

Pierre J. Mejlak was born on the Mediterranean island of Malta in 1982. His story collections are *I Am Waiting for You to Fall with the Rain* and *What the Night Lets You Say*. He has won five Malta National Book Awards and in 2014 won the European Union Prize for Literature. He lives in Brussels.

Margarita Meklina is a Russian novelist and story writer considered groundbreaking in her prose, which helped redefine Russian literature in the 1990s. She has published five books and has won many awards; she was nominated for The Russian Prize in 2009. She lives in San Francisco.

Czesław Miłosz, who died in 2004, was a Polish poet and prose writer of Lithuanian origin. "Esse" is usually assumed to be a prose poem, but it has also been noted as a "perfect flash love story." Miłosz won the Nobel Prize in 1980.

Augusto Monterroso was an important figure in the Latin American "boom" generation; his story "Dinosaur" is said to have started the micro fiction movement. He received some of the highest literature and humanities awards in Guatemala, Mexico, and Spain. He died in 2003.

Ibrahim Muhawi is a renowned Palestinian social scientist and translator of many books, including (as coauthor) *Speak Bird, Speak Again: Palestinian Arab Folktales*. He studied English literature at the University of California, Berkeley and was director of the master's program in translation studies at the University of Edinburgh.

Edward Mullany is the author of *If I Falter at the Gallows* and *Figures for an Apocalypse*. He grew up in Australia and in the American Midwest.

Shabnam Nadiya grew up in Jahangirnagar, a small college campus in Bangladesh. She is a recent graduate of and a Schulze Fellow at the Iowa Writers' Workshop, and is working on a collection of linked stories called *Pariah Dog and Other Stories*.

María Negroni has published two novels and several books of poetry, one of which won the Argentine National Book Award. She has taught at Sarah Lawrence College since 1999 and is now directing the first creative writing program in Argentina.

Stefani Nellen is from Germany, but spent many years in the United States, and now lives in the Netherlands with her husband, a Dutchman. She is writing two novels, and her short stories have been published in various literary magazines; she won first prize in the *Glimmer Train* Fiction Open.

Kirk Nesset is the author of *Paradise Road* and *Mr. Agreeable* (fiction), as well as *Saint X* (poetry), *Alphabet of the World* (translation), and *The Stories of Raymond Carver* (nonfiction). His work has appeared in *The Paris Review*, *The Southern Review*, *The Kenyon Review*, *The American Poetry Review*, *Gettysburg Review*, *Witness*, and *Ploughshares*.

James Norcliffe is a New Zealand poet who has also published short fiction, as well as several novels for young people, including the award-winning *The Loblolly Boy* (published in the United States as *The Boy Who Could Fly*).

Giannis Palavos was born in Velventos, Kozani in Greece in 1980. He studied journalism at Aristotle University in Thessaloniki and arts administration at the Panteion University in Athens. He is widely recognized as one of Greece's best new writers. His short stories have won prizes from the British Council and *Anagnostis* magazine and most recently the Greek National Book Award.

Edmundo Paz Soldán is the author of fourteen books of fiction and winner of Bolivia's National Book Award and the Juan Rulfo Award; he is also an essayist, journalist, translator, and coeditor with Alberto Fuguet of an anthology of new Latin American fiction, *Se habla español*. He teaches at Cornell University.

Petronius was a Roman consul in the time of Nero. The post of consul had little authority, but he was popular, according to the historian Tacitus, for his reckless freedom of speech. He is best known as the author of a satirical novel, *The Satyricon*, which was the basis of Fellini's 1969 movie of the same name.

Virgilio Piñera was born in Cárdenas, Cuba, and died in Havana in 1979. His work includes several collections of stories, notably *Cuentos frios* (*Cold Tales*); his other works include essays on literature and literary criticism, numerous dramatic works, and three novels.

Robert Pinsky is the author of two translated books, *The Inferno of Dante* and *The Separate Notebooks: Poems by Czeslaw Milosz*. He has also published numerous collections of poetry as well as nonfiction books and was U.S. Poet Laureate from 1997 to 2000. He teaches in the graduate creative writing program at Boston University.

Meg Pokrass writes flash fiction, short stories, and poetry. Her first collection of flash fiction is *Damn Sure Straight*. Her work has appeared in many literary magazines; she is editor-at-large for *BLIP Magazine* (formerly *Mississippi Review*). She lives in San Francisco.

Lili Potpara, born in Maribor, Slovenia, is a writer and freelance translator. Her story collection *Zgodbe na dusek* (*Bottoms Up Stories*) won the best literary debut award at the 2002 Slovenian Book Fair. A mother of two, Lili holds a B.A. in French and English from the University of Ljubljana.

Shouhua Qi is the author of *Red Guard Fantasies and Other Stories* and *When the Purple Mountain Burns*; editor and translator of *The Pearl Jacket and Other Stories: Flash Fiction from Contemporary China*; and coauthor of *Voices in Tragic Harmony: Essays on Thomas Hardy's Fiction and Poetry*. He came to the United States from China in 1989 and is a professor of English at Western Connecticut State University.

Qiu Xiaolong was born in Shanghai, China. He is a poet, literary translator, crime novelist, critic, and academic living in St. Louis, Missouri, with his wife and daughter. He originally visited the United States in 1988 to write a book about T. S. Eliot, but following the Tiananmen Square protests of 1989 he was forced to remain in the United States to avoid persecution. His books have sold over a million copies and have been translated into twenty languages.

Shirani Rajapakse is a Sri Lankan poet and author whose work has appeared in many journals. Her collection of short stories, *Breaking News*, was shortlisted for the Gratiaen Prize.

Kristina Zdravič Reardon is a writer, translator, and doctoral candidate in comparative literary and cultural studies at the University of Connecticut. She holds an MFA in fiction writing from the University of New Hampshire and in 2010 was awarded a Fulbright grant to study translation in Slovenia.

Lesley Riva is the translator of *Friendly Fire: The Remarkable Story of a Journalist Kidnapped in Iraq, Rescued by an Italian Secret Service Agent, and Shot by U.S. Forces.* She is also the author of books and articles on interior design, food, travel, and family.

Bruce Holland Rogers is a writer and teacher whose stories have won a Pushcart Prize, Nebula, Bram Stoker, World Fantasy, and Micro Awards, and have been nominated for the Edgar Allan Poe Award and Spain's Premio Ignotus. The short film *The Other Side*, directed by Mary Stuart Masterson, was based on his novelette, *Lifeboat on a Burning Sea*.

Ethel Rohan has two award-winning story collections, *Goodnight Nobody* and *Cut Through the Bone*. Her work has appeared in publications such as *The New York Times*, *World Literature Today*, *Tin House Online*, and the *Irish Times*. Raised in Ireland, she now lives in San Francisco.

Josephine Rowe is an Australian writer of short fiction, poetry, and essays. Her collections include *How a Moth Becomes a Boat* and

Tarcutta Wake, and her stories have appeared in *Meanjin*, *The Iowa Review*, *Harvard Review*, and *McSweeney's*. She is a 2014–16 Stegner Fellow in fiction at Stanford University.

Eric Rugara is a young man in his twenties living in Nairobi, Kenya. Writing is his foremost passion. His influences have been Ngugi wa Thiong'o, Peter Abrahams, and Ernest Hemingway, to name a few. With this, his first major breakthrough, he hopes to begin a fruitful career in letters.

Juan José Saer was one of the most important Argentine writers of the last fifty years. He grew up in rural Argentina, and in 1968 moved to Paris, where he lived until his death in 2005. His body of work includes twelve novels, four collections of short stories, and one poetry collection; several of his stories have been made into movies.

Robert Scotellaro was born and raised in New York City and once played bongos onstage as Allen Ginsberg recited poetry. His stories and poems have appeared widely; he has published five chapbooks and a full-length book of flash fiction, *Measuring the Distance*. He now lives in San Francisco with his wife, his daughter, and his writing companion, a real cool dog named Addie.

Daryl Scroggins (see his story in Flash Theory) is the author of *This Is Not the Way We Came In*. His short stories have appeared in many magazines; his books are *The Game of Kings* and *Winter Investments*, a collection of short stories; his work *Prairie Shapes*, a Flash Novel, won the 2004 Robert J. DeMott Prose Contest. He lives in Marfa, Texas.

Gwen Shapard works for a nonprofit that teaches ESL and Spanish literacy to immigrants. She has degrees from Trinity University in San Antonio and the University of Texas at Austin.

H. J. Shepard writes poetry and short stories. Raised in Minnesota, she is a historian of the American West. She lives in New York.

Ana María Shua is an award-winning Argentinean writer who is often referred to as "the Queen of the Microstory." She has published over eighty books in numerous genres, and her stories appear in anthologies throughout the world. Several books of her short-short stories have been published in the United States recently, including *Microfictions* and *Without a Net*.

Katherine Silver is an award-winning translator of Spanish and Latin American literature and the codirector of the Banff International Literary Translation Centre. Her many translations include a collection of modern and contemporary Chilean fiction, as well as plays, screenplays for major motion pictures, and works of nonfiction.

Jethro Soutar is a Lisbon-based translator of Portuguese and Spanish. He has translated books for Bitter Lemon Press and And Other Stories, and recently cotranslated and edited *The Football Crónicas*.

Peter Stamm was born and raised in Switzerland. He studied in many fields, was an intern at a psychiatric clinic, and after living in New York, Paris, and Scandinavia became a writer and freelance journalist in Zurich. He has published numerous books of prose, as well as plays and radio dramas.

Steven J. Stewart has published books of translations of the work of Rafael Pérez Estrada (Spain), Fernando Iwasaki (Peru), and Ana María Shua (Argentina). He was awarded a 2005 Literature Fellowship for Translation by the National Endowment for the Arts and was a finalist for the 2005 PEN USA translation award.

Raymond Stock is an American writer, scholar, translator, musician, and actor who lived in Cairo for twenty years. Among his specialties are the Middle East and Arabic-English translation. He has translated seven books and numerous stories by Egyptian Nobel laureate Naguib Mahfouz and is writing a biography of Mahfouz.

Ricardo Sumalavia, born in Lima, is a professor at the Catholic University of Peru and coordinator of its Center for Oriental Studies. He is the author of three story collections: *Habitaciones* (Rooms); *Retratos familiares* (Family Portraits); *Enciclopedia mínima* (Minimal Encyclopedia); and the novel *Que la tierra te sea leve* (May the Earth Lie Lightly Upon You). He teaches at the Université Michel de Montaigne, in Bordeaux, France.

Karina M. Szczurek was born in Poland, studied in Austria and Wales, and moved to South Africa in 2005. She is a writer, editor, and literary critic. Her first novel, *Invisible Others*, was published in 2014. She lives in Cape Town with her husband, André Brink.

Zakaria Tamer of Syria is one of the most important and widely read and translated short story writers in the Arab world. His works include twelve story collections. Many of his stories are flash length.

James Tate has many awards in poetry, including the William Carlos Williams Award, the Pulitzer Prize, and the National Book Award. He also has several books of prose; his story "Farewell, I Love You, and Goodbye" comes from *Dreams of a Robot Dancing Bee: 44 Stories*.

Penelope Todd has authored several novels, most for young adults (notably the *Watermark* trilogy), a bilingually written and published novel, *Amigas*, with Elena Bossi, and a memoir, *Digging for*

Spain: A Writer's Journey. She works as a writer and editor and is New Zealand's first independent ebook publisher at Rosa Mira Books.

Anne Twitty writes, translates, and interprets in and in-between languages and traditions. She received the PEN Prize for Poetry in Translation in 2002 and an NEA translation grant in 2006. She is coauthor with Iraj Anvar of *Say Nothing: Poems of Jalal al-Din Rumi.*

Antonio Ungar, born in 1974, is the author of two short story collections and the novels *Las orejas del lobo,* shortlisted for the Courier International Prize for the best foreign book published in France in 2008, and *Tres ataúdes blancos,* winner of the Herralde Prize in 2010, shortlisted for the Rómulo Gallegos Prize in 2011 and translated into ten languages.

Karen Van Dyck teaches and directs Modern Greek Studies in the Classics Department at Columbia University. Her translations include *The Rehearsal of Misunderstanding: Three Collections by Contemporary Greek Women Poets, The Scattered Papers of Penelope: New and Selected Poems by Katerina Anghelaki-Rooke,* and *The Greek Poets: Homer to the Present.*

Juan Villoro is the Mexican author of many books, including novels and short story collections. He has been well known within intellectual circles in Mexico, Latin America, and Spain for years, but his success among readers grew after he received the Herralde Prize for his novel *El testigo.*

Natasha Wimmer is an American translator of Spanish literature that includes Roberto Bolaño's *2666* (which won the National Book Award and the PEN Translation Prize) and *The Savage Detectives*; and three novels by Mario Vargas Llosa.

Bess Winter grew up in Toronto and has lived in Kansas City; Victoria, British Columbia; Sackville, New Brunswick; and Bowling Green, Ohio. Her story "Signs" won a 2013 Pushcart Prize and the American Short(er) Fiction Award; others appear in *Indiana Review, American Short Fiction, Versal, Berkeley Fiction Review,* and *Wigleaf.* She is a Ph.D. student at the University of Cincinnati.

Sholeh Wolpé is a poet, literary translator, and fiction writer. Born in Iran, in her teen years she lived in Trinidad and the United Kingdom, before settling in the United States. Her work has won the Midwest Book Award and Lois Roth Persian Translation Prize, and has been translated into several languages.

Mohibullah Zegham was born in 1973 in Kabul, Afghanistan. He first wrote fiction in 2005 when he was working as a physician in Kajaki, a war-torn district of Helmand province in the south. A year later, his first collection of short stories was published by the PEN Society of Afghanistan. He now has ten books.

CREDITS

Natasza Goerke, "Stories," translated by W. Martin, originally appeared in *Farewells to Plasma*, published in 2001 by Twisted Spoon Press, Prague. Reprinted by permission of the publisher.

Judd Hampton, "Three-Second Angels," first published in *Smokelong Quarterly*, no. 7, is reprinted by permission of the author.

Tania Hershman, "The Heavy Bones," from *The White Road and Other Stories* (Salt Publishing Limited, 2009), is reprinted by permission of the publisher.

Randa Jarrar, "A Sailor," published in *Guernica*/PEN Flash Series Online, is reprinted by permission of the author.

Franz Kafka, "An Imperial Message," translated by Ian Johnston, Vancouver Island University. Reprinted by permission of the translator.

Etgar Keret, "The Story, Victorious" and "The Story, Victorious II," from *Suddenly, a Knock on the Door*, translated by Miriam Shlesinger, Sondra Silverston, and Nathan Englander. English translation copyright © 2012 by Etgar Keret. Reprinted by permission of Farrar, Straus and Giroux, LLC and Atiken Alexander Associates, Ltd.

Kim Young-ha, "Honor Killing," translated by Chi-Young Kim, was first published in *Esquire* online, Napkin Fiction, April 16, 2008. Reprinted by permission of Lippincott Massie McQuilkin as agents for the author and by permission of the translator. Copyright © Kim Young-ha.

Tara Laskowski, "Little Girls," from *Smokelong Quarterly*, no. 26, is reprinted by permission of the author.

Mónica Lavín, "Volcanic Fireflies," is translated by Patricia Dubrava. Reprinted by permission of the author and translator.

Kirsty Logan, "The Light Eater," from *The Rental Heart and Other Fairytales* (Salt Publishing, 2014), is reprinted by permission of the publisher.

Robert Lopez, "Everyone Out Of the Pool," published in *Mid-American Review* (2012), is reprinted by permission of the author.

Antonio López-Ortega, "Trilogy," from *Moonlit* (1999), translated by Nathan Budoff, is reprinted by permission of Brookline Books.

Naguib Mahfouz, from *The Dreams*, copyright © 2000–2003 by Naguib Mahfouz. English translation copyright © 2004 by Raymond Stock. Used by permission of the American University in Cairo Press.

Luigi Malerba, "Consuming the View," translated by Lesley Riva from *Italian Tales*, edited by Massimo Riva (Yale University Press, 2005), is reprinted by permission of the translator and the Estate of Luigi Malerba.

Giorgio Manganelli, "An Ouroboric Novel," appears as "#75" in *Centuria: One Hundred Ouroboric Novels* (McPherson & Co., 2007), translated by Henry Martin. Reprinted by permission of the publisher.

Kuzhali Manickavel, "Everyone Does Integral Calculus," is reprinted by permission of the author.

W. Somerset Maugham, "Appointment in Samarra," epigraph from *Sheppey*. Reprinted by permission of United Agents on behalf of the Literary Fund.

Karina Magdalena Szczurek, "Not Far From the Tree," first published in *Flash: The International Short-Short Story Magazine*, vol. 2, no. 1, 2009, is reprinted by permission of the author.

Zakaria Tamer, "The Five New Sons," by Zakaria Tamer, translated by Ibrahim Muhawi, from *Breaking Knees* (2008), pp. 45–47. Reprinted by permission of the publisher Garnet Publishing.

James Tate, "Farewell, I Love You, and Goodbye," from *Dreams of a Robot Dancing Bee*. Copyright © 2002 by James Tate. Published by Verse Press. Reprinted with permission of Wave Books.

Antonio Ungar, "Honey," is reprinted by permission of the author.

Juan Villoro, "The Voice of the Enemy," translated by George Henson, is reprinted by permission of the author and the translator.

Bess Winter, "Signs," is reprinted by permission of the author.

Sholeh Wolpé, "My Brother at the Canadian Border," from *The Scar Saloon* (2004) is reprinted by permission of the publisher Red Hen Press.

Yasunari Kawabata, "Sleeping Habit," from *Palm-of-the-Hand Stories*, translated by Lane Dunlop and J. Martin Holman. Translation copyright © 1988 by Lane Dunlop and J. Martin Holman. Reprinted by permission of North Point Press, a division of Farrar, Straus and Giroux LLC.

Yin Ee Kiong, "Ronggeng," is reprinted by permission of the author.

Mohibulla Zegham, "The Tiger," as translated by Rashid Khattak. Reprinted by permission of the author and translator.

ABOUT THE EDITORS

CHRISTOPHER MERRILL is the author of many books, most recently *Boat* (poetry), *Necessities* (prose poetry), and *The Tree of the Doves: Ceremony, Expedition, War* (nonfiction). He is also a translator of several volumes and editor of many others. He directs the International Writing Program at the University of Iowa.

ROBERT SHAPARD has coedited seven books of very short fiction, including *Flash Fiction Forward, Sudden Fiction International,* and *Sudden Fiction Latino,* and cofounded *Mānoa: A Pacific Journal of International Writing.* His own stories have won national awards; his flash chapbook is *Motel and Other Stories.*

JAMES THOMAS has coedited all of the *Flash Fiction* and *Sudden Fiction* books. He is the founder of *Quarterly West* and the annual Writers@Work Conference. He has received a Stegner Fellowship from Stanford, a James Michener Fellowship, and two NEA grants. His story collection is *Pictures, Moving.*